The Matchmaking Pact
Carolyne Aarsen

Steeple
Hill®

Published by Steeple Hill Books™

Special thanks and acknowledgment to Carolyne Aarsen for her contribution to the After the Storm miniseries.

STEEPLE HILL BOOKS

Steeple Hill®

Recycling programs for this product may not exist in your area.

ISBN-13: 978-0-373-87554-2

THE MATCHMAKING PACT

**It had been six years since Josie had
a man over for supper.**

Six years since her responsibilities completely
changed the course of her life. Six years since she
carried Alyssa away from the hospital, a confused
little girl of two, an orphan, with only her aunt Josie
to take care of her.

An aunt who up until then had lived life on her own
terms. Josie's life had taken a 180-degree turn, and
there were many times since then that she thanked
God for a second chance to redeem herself. Both in
His eyes and in the eyes of the community.

She was determined to be a good mother to Alyssa,
to focus solely on the little girl and her needs.

And now a man's voice reverberated from the living
room. A man was joining them for dinner. And not
just any man: Silas Marstow.

After the Storm:
A Kansas community unites to rebuild

Books by Carolyne Aarsen

Love Inspired

Homecoming
Ever Faithful
A Bride at Last
The Cowboy's Bride
*A Family-Style Christmas
*A Mother at Heart
*A Family at Last
A Hero for Kelsey
Twin Blessings
Toward Home
Love Is Patient
A Heart's Refuge
Brought Together by Baby
A Silence in the Heart
Any Man of Mine
Yuletide Homecoming
Finally a Family
A Family for Luke
The Matchmaking Pact

*Stealing Home

CAROLYNE AARSEN

and her husband, Richard, live on a small ranch in Northern Alberta, where they have raised four children and numerous foster children, and are still raising cattle. Carolyne crafts her stories in her office with a large west-facing window, through which she can watch the changing seasons while struggling to make her words obey.

Come to me all you who are weary
and burdened and I will give you rest.
—*Matthew* 11:28

To those whose lives have been torn apart
by storms—without and within

Prologue

July 10, 5:00 p.m.

"Alyssa. Lily." Josie threw the young girls' names out into the eerie quiet blanketing the town of High Plains.

The quiet that was the aftermath of the tornado.

She took a quick step down the church steps and called out again.

An hour ago her ears had ached from the roaring rush of wind, the screech of wood being pulled free from the nails, the distinctive sound of a roaring train that came with the tornado ripping through the late afternoon.

An hour ago she had held her niece, Alyssa, and Alyssa's best friend, Lily, close to her side while the storm raged overhead. Half an hour ago, as frantic parents came to check on the children in Josie's care, Lily and Alyssa were still around. But since that time, as calm began to return, the two girls had disappeared.

"Lily. Alyssa." She yelled louder this time, as her panicked gaze flicked over the devastation the tornado had wrought, disbelief and sorrow flooding over her.

Tree branches the size of her arm lay on the street, chunks

of plywood, splintered timbers and unrecognizable debris littered a landscape she no longer recognized.

The Old Town Hall, one of the first buildings put up in High Plains all those years ago, was nothing more than a jumble of broken wood and windows, as if someone had picked it up and dropped it, with no regard for its history or its place in the town.

So close, she thought, fear clutching her midsection at the sight. The tornado that had ripped the Old Town Hall to rubble had—like the Egyptian Angel of Death—passed over the church doing nothing more than pulling down a sign.

She breathed another prayer, a mixture of gratitude for her safety and supplication for those who might be hurt as she struggled to absorb the wreckage of her town.

A few people stood in front of the businesses lining the street, their faces as dazed as—Josie was sure—hers was at what had just happened.

Where in all of this had her niece gone with her new best friend, Lily Marstow? And why had they left when Josie had specifically told them to stay close?

When they had asked if they could go to the washroom, Josie had watched them go, then a little girl crying for her mother had caught her attention.

Ten minutes had passed before she realized the girls weren't with her friend Nicki or anywhere in the church. Nor had anyone seen them.

Dear Lord, please let them be okay, she prayed as she stepped out into the wet street littered with branches, wood and hunks of soggy pink insulation.

What had she been thinking letting them even step out of her sight?

She hadn't. She'd been too busy listening to the stories that came with each new person coming to claim their child from the preschool at the church.

And she'd been too busy trying to call her own grandmother who lived a few blocks away, hoping, praying the elderly woman was safe. But neither the phones nor her cell phone worked. She had no idea what had happened to her grandmother and, up until now, hadn't dared venture out to find out.

"Alyssa. Lily. If you can hear me, you better be coming back to the church this second." Josie tried to keep her voice firm and steady but it wobbled on the last few words.

She was going to tan their silly, irresponsible hides when she found them.

"Did you find them?" her friend Nicki called from the top of the church steps, the worry in her voice adding to Josie's.

"No. I have no idea where to start looking." Josie hugged herself, the wreckage of the town slowly impressing itself upon her weary brain. She was sure she would remember the roar, the fury and the howling rush of wind until she died.

"And I'm worried about my grandmother. I can't get hold of her. I don't know what to do first."

Nicki joined her friend and gave her a one-armed hug. "Reverend Garrison's niece Avery is still here. I can ask her to see what she can find out."

"That would be great."

"Reverend Garrison told me emergency crews are coming, too."

Josie nodded, her eyes scanning the devastation hoping for a glimpse of either girl.

Across the street Tom Driessen stood in front of his pizza place, still wearing his white apron tied around his generous girth. Glass from the window of his business covered the street.

"Are you okay, Mr. Driessen?" Josie asked as she ran down the stairs.

"Yeah. But look at my place. What am I going to do? What are we all going to do?"

She wanted to help, but she had a more pressing mission. "Did you see two, little, eight-year-old girls? They both have red hair, green eyes. One was wearing a pink T-shirt and green shorts, the other a lemon-yellow sundress." Josie had sewn the sundress herself and had just finished putting the buttons on it this morning, just before school.

"The twins?"

"Yeah." Josie didn't take time to correct him. The girls looked so much alike, this had been a common mistake from the day Lily was enrolled in school in High Plains.

"I was just cleaning up inside when I saw them go by." Tom ran his hand over his face. He looked so tired.

"Which way did they go?" Josie tried to keep the panic out of her voice. She had to stay calm and rational.

"That way." As soon as Tom pointed down Fourth Street, Josie knew exactly where Alyssa and Lily had gone.

"Thanks. Take care," she said, her words an inadequate response. There was so much to do, she thought, the wreckage of the town overwhelming her. How would they get through this? Where would they start?

Focus, Josie. First you need to find Alyssa.

And Silas Marstow's daughter.

The thought of facing that impassive face with the news that his daughter was missing was almost as frightening as the tornado itself.

Since losing his wife two years ago, Silas Marstow had virtually become a recluse on his farm. He was also extremely protective of his only child. He had reluctantly put Lily in Josie's after-school-care program two weeks ago and only because he had some extra work to do on his ranch, according to Alyssa.

If he were to find out his daughter had disappeared from Josie's after-school program right after a horrific storm had ripped through the town...

Josie hugged herself, still chilly from her reaction to the storm. She couldn't remember ever being so afraid.

And the last time she had prayed this much was after hearing the news of her sister's and brother-in-law's deaths.

A deep voice called her name and Josie's already over-worked heart tripped into overdrive.

She turned to see Silas running down the street, his long legs eating up the distance between them.

He stopped in front of her, his eyebrows two slashes over deep-set eyes flashing his disapproval, his square jaw clenched in anger. "I just stopped at the church and they told me Lily wasn't there." His voice was an angry wave washing over her, but guilt and fear kept her tongue-tied.

Silas caught Josie by the shoulders. "Where's Lily? Where's my daughter?"

"She and Alyssa slipped out," she managed to squeak out.

"What?" Silas's grip on her shoulders increased, his pale brown eyes drilling into her. "You're supposed to be taking care of her. I heard the reports, I saw the cloud, the storm. I came as soon as I could."

"They only left a few minutes ago. Lily and my niece. I'm pretty sure I know where they are."

"Pretty sure? That's not good enough." His eyes narrowed and he gave her a shake, as if trying to force the information out of her. "This town, this place…" His gruff voice drifted away as his gaze shot around, as if trying to take in the havoc around them.

A burst of wind, a remnant of the raging storm, tossed her long blond hair about her face. And as she pushed it back, her arm hit his. "If you'll let go of me, I'll go with you to find the girls."

"Let's go, then," he growled, dropping his hands.

Josie turned blindly, her own fear and concern mixing with the shame she felt at letting the girls slip out of her sight at such a time.

Irresponsible. Reckless. The words her grandmother often tossed her way now slithered through her mind, resurrecting a wild past that still accused her.

She shouldn't be in charge of these children. She couldn't take care of them.

Please, Lord, let them be okay. She prayed through her fear and through the voices from her past that told her she was no good. Worthless and nothing but trouble.

But in spite of her prayers, fear clenched her stomach as she navigated her way over a downed tree. Beyond that an empty car lay on its side, glass strewn over a street still wet from the rain. It had been half an hour since the tornado touched down. While she and Nicki had cowered with the children in the basement of the church, sirens had wailed and horns honked, followed by the roar of the storm filling their ears and minds.

Another tree lay across their path, and as she tried to go over it, as well, her foot got caught in the branches. She would have fallen but for Silas's strong hands catching her from behind.

"I'm okay. Let go of me," she snapped. Fear, anger with Alyssa and concern about her grandmother fought with each other as she struggled to free herself from the branches and the grip of his rough hands.

"Just a minute." Silas snapped a few branches away, vaulted over the tree, then reached up to help her down, but she scrambled down on her own.

"Where are we going?" he asked as she caught her balance.

"If my guess is right, the girls went to my house. Go down Fourth to Logan Street. I live two houses down from the corner."

Without another word Silas strode away from her. "Watch out for the downed power lines," he called over his shoulder as his long legs covered ground. As Josie jogged to keep up, her gaze flew around the town taking stock. The Willekers house okay, but the stately maples destroyed. Roof off Klaas Steenbergen's house. Windows smashed in the next house. The following house, no damage.

Then they turned onto Logan Street, and Josie's steps faltered.

The capricious tornado had blasted out the windows of the homes on either side of her and snatched branches off the maples that had once lined the street.

And tossed them right into the front of her house.

Her roof was a bundle of sticks and shingles burying the front porch and lawn. One side of the house was ripped right out, exposing her living room and part of the kitchen, which now held only a kitchen chair and her new television tipped on its side.

The sound of sirens approaching broke into the silence that had held the town in thrall up to now. Emergency vehicles on their way.

Panic clawed up Josie's throat as the demolition of her home dawned on her. Did the girls go inside that mess?

She ran toward the house, ignoring Silas's warning shout. *Please, Lord,* was all she could pray.

"Josie. Stop. Now. There's a line down."

He snaked his arm around her waist to stop her forward momentum.

A power line sparked only inches away from her feet.

Fear made Josie sag against Silas. For a brief moment she welcomed the strength of his arm holding her up, the solid wall of his body behind her.

Then, above the sound of emergency sirens approaching, Josie heard Alyssa calling her name.

"Wait here," Silas said, releasing her.

Josie hugged herself, praying frantically as Silas carefully made his way over the downed power line then through the debris on the lawn to the back of the house. He called the girls' names as Josie prayed. *Please, Lord, let those girls be safe.*

After what seemed like an eternity, Silas came from behind the house, his daughter on his hip, his other hand holding Alyssa's.

Alyssa was carrying a plastic bag, but Josie was too relieved to pay it much attention.

She ran toward her niece and swept her into her arms.

"You silly girl. I was so worried." She dropped to her knees, her hands slipping over her niece's dear face. "Are you okay? What were you thinking leaving like that?"

Alyssa glanced at Lily, then back at Josie. "I wanted to get something. From the house. For Lily."

Fear and anger fought for dominance, but relief took the upper hand.

"Why didn't you ask me? Why did you go without telling me? Do you know what just happened?"

Alyssa looked around and sighed. "The storm left a big mess."

Her simple, matter-of-fact statement released some of Josie's tension.

"It was very dangerous to go to the house without telling me." Josie's voice trembled.

"I'm sorry. But now I have my present for Lily. I had it ready in the kitchen but forgot it." Alyssa glanced up at Silas. "Are we going to the church? I want to wrap it there. I have some pretty paper."

Silas shifted his daughter on his hip, his tanned forearms holding her close as he shot a frown toward Josie. "No. I'm taking Lily home. Now."

Lily pushed back on her father, her tiny hands dwarfed by her father's broad shoulders. "I want my present."

Silas's angry gaze flicked around the wreckage strewn about the street, as if wondering how his daughter could be so caught up in something so trivial as a present when people's lives had been upended so dramatically.

"Can you give it to her now?" Silas asked Alyssa.

Alyssa glanced at the plastic bag holding something square. Then as the emergency vehicles converged on their street, red and blue light strobing over the street, she handed the parcel to Lily.

"Happy birthday, Lily," she said with a wide smile.

Josie saw Silas's face go blank, then he closed his eyes and pulled his lower lip between his teeth.

The single father had forgotten his only daughter's birthday.

"Thanks, Alyssa," Lily said with a huge grin, seemingly unaware of her father's mistake. Then she turned to Silas. "Can Alyssa and Miss Cane come over for a party?"

Silas shot a glance over his shoulder at the remains of Josie's house, something she'd been avoiding ever since they turned down this street.

"I think Ms. Cane has other things on her mind right now." Silas put Lily down, but clung to her hand. He looked around the street as one of the emergency crews ran to the house beside Josie's and another to hers.

"There's no one inside," Josie called out. "We're both here."

One of the firemen saluted her, but followed the other man in anyhow.

Guess they had to check for themselves, she reasoned.

She turned away, unable to look at the wreckage any longer. Later she could absorb it, reason what had to happen. For now, she had to find out what had happened to her grandmother.

"We gotta get going," Silas said, shoving his hand through his hair, as if unsure himself what to do. "Glad that you and the girls are okay." He gave her a tight smile, then walked down the littered street, leading his daughter by the hand.

Josie watched him go as a hard shivering seized her body.

Shock, she reasoned, hugging herself. She tried to keep her thoughts at bay, tried to corral them into a corner.

But they buzzed past her defenses. Was her grandmother okay? Who else could have been hurt?

"I have to go find Gramma," Josie said suddenly.

"Do you think she's okay?"

"We'll find out." She was about to leave when a fireman called her back.

"Ma'am, we have to ask you to head back to the church." He walked over to her full of purpose and determination. "We're sending everyone there for now."

"But my grandmother…"

"We'll be giving out news as we find things out. It's too dangerous to go wandering the streets on your own. Gas leaks, lines down. Sorry."

Josie hugged herself again, glancing over her shoulder in the direction of her grandmother's home.

This storm had changed everything. It had blasted into town, torn up homes, and even though it had happened only an hour ago, Josie knew it had completely rearranged her life and her plans.

Guess she wouldn't be moving away from High Plains this fall after all.

Two days later

"So what are we going to do, Lily?" Alyssa pressed her mouth close to her aunt's cell phone, hoping Aunt Josie hadn't noticed that Alyssa was missing from the classroom in the church. If Aunt Josie knew she was using her cell phone, and why, she would be mad. "If you're not allowed to come to the after-school program anymore, how is my aunt and your dad going to fall in love like we planned?"

"We need to make a pact."

"Is that a sin?"

"No, silly." Lily laughed. "It's a promise that you and I are going to make to make sure that my dad and your aunt fall in love."

"Like a pact. A matchmaking pact."

"Yeah. A pact."

"But we have to hurry because my aunt still says we're going to move away. And if we move, they're never going to fall in love." Alyssa looked back over her shoulder, but no one was in the hallway. "So we're going to make a pact and make a plan."

"Right. And this is what we'll do."

Alyssa listened carefully and as Lily told her the plan, she started to smile. This might work. And if it did, she would have a dad again.

And Lily would get another mom.

Chapter One

October 5th

"Lily. Time for school," Silas called up the stairs, waiting for a response from his daughter.

He heard a thump, then the sound of feet hurrying down the hallway. What in the world was that kid doing? Curious, he took a step up the stairs just as his cell phone rang.

He pulled it off his hip and flipped it open. A modern-day gunslinger, he thought with a touch of irony as he said hello.

"Silas. Orville Cummins here. Not the best news. I've got to delay shipping that lumber to you."

"What do you mean? I ordered it back in June for delivery this month."

"Yeah. That was before that tornado took your town apart couple months back. I tried to get what I could, but Garrison has been buying up what he can for his lumberyard the last while. You could try to get some from him."

Silas rubbed his forehead. "He's only selling it for reconstruction or building new homes."

"If you can wait two weeks, I'll get you what you need from Manhattan."

"I guess that'll have to do."

As he was talking, Lily came downstairs, dragging her backpack behind her, a brightly colored gift bag swinging from her other hand.

While he talked he wiped a spot of toothpaste from the corner of Lily's mouth, then patted her on the head.

"Thanks again, Orville. I gotta run." He snapped the phone shut and slipped it into his belt holster. "Did you really brush your teeth this morning or only rinse with toothpaste again?"

"I brushed."

Silas frowned at her ponytail, hanging askew from the back of her head.

Kelly would have put their daughter's copper-colored hair into tight, fat braids, finished off with ribbons.

But Kelly wasn't here and his clumsy fingers couldn't re-create the intricate twists that had come so easily to his wife's slender fingers. So Lily did her own hair. Today it looked as if she hadn't even brushed it.

"We gotta get going." He glanced at the festive bag she was carrying. "What you got there?"

Lily gave him a secretive smile. "You'll find out."

"Okay. Secrets. Very intriguing."

The drive into town was quiet. Silas was lost in his thoughts, the only sound in the truck the ticking of gravel on the undercarriage and the nasally twang of the announcer from the early-morning stock market report on the radio. He had a lot to do in the next few weeks and the time was slipping through his fingers.

"Dad, can we have a puppy?" Lily's voice broke into the quiet.

"A puppy?" Where in the world had that come from? "I've got enough trouble keeping you groomed and fed." He tossed Lily a grin, just to show he was kidding.

"But a puppy would keep me company. When you're busy."

"I'm not that busy, honey."

"You're outside all the time and when you're not, you're on the computer. And I hate watching television."

That sent a shot of guilt through him. Kelly had hated television, too, and had limited how much Lily watched. But television kept Lily occupied and out of his hair while he worked.

"Why can't I go to the after-school program instead? With my friend Alyssa?" Lily clutched the shiny bag that Silas suspected held a present for that same friend.

"Because, honey" was all he would say.

He couldn't explain to her the sheer terror he had felt when he'd seen the funnel cloud touch down in High Plains, knowing she was there instead of on the farm where she'd have been safe.

A thousand images of Lily hurt, or worse, had sliced through his head on that panicked trip into town. He'd even been tempted to pray.

Which was foolishness, of course. God hadn't heard the countless prayers he and Lily had sent up for Kelly during her battle with cancer. When he and his sobbing daughter had stood by her graveside, Silas had promised himself he wouldn't waste God's time anymore.

"I miss seeing Ms. Josie," Lily put in, still campaigning.

"Miss Cane let you and Alyssa take off after the tornado. She's not responsible."

That Lily had been found safe was no thanks to Miss Cane, who had let her and her friend slip out in the first place.

Lily sighed again. "I hate sitting by myself at home, Daddy."

More guilt piled onto his shoulders.

"It was Alyssa's idea to sneak out when we had that tornado, you know."

"Which is another reason you shouldn't be hanging around with Alyssa." This conversation was well-tilled ground. But his daughter was persistent and each time approached it from another angle as if hoping to unearth some new argument to convince him.

"But she's my twin friend. And she has a really pretty aunt."

Silas wasn't about to dispute the pretty-aunt part of her statement. Josie Cane was the kind of woman who would make any man look twice and then again. Tall with blond hair rivalling ripe Kansas grain and a smile inviting a response.

And a reputation that preceded her.

It was a good thing he wasn't looking and he wasn't interested. The long, slow loss of his wife, Kelly, had squeezed his heart to nothing. When the first clumps of dirt were dropped on her coffin, his heart had closed like a fist on his memories and his pain. He hadn't talked about Kelly nor encouraged Lily to do the same. He was tired of hurt and pain.

"Doesn't matter how pretty she is." Silas made his voice gruff to show Lily he was serious. "I want you home."

Where I can make sure you're safe, he added to himself.

"But Alyssa told me that Ms. Josie is doing baking at the church. For the workers who are building the town again. Ms. Josie said we all have to do our part and I want to help, too. I want to learn how to bake, then I can make cupcakes and muffins, like Mommy used to."

In spite of the sadness the memories brought, Silas had to smile. Kelly was wonder and joy and love, but she was no baker. Each attempt created a potential health hazard.

"And I won't be so lonely after school when you're doing all your work," she continued, her voice growing earnest. "And you won't have to keep checking on me. Ms. Josie said she'd gladly take me back again."

Silas was wavering. He had a ton of work to do today and he had already been juggling his timelines, trying to figure out how he was supposed to stop what he was doing in time to pick Lily up from school every day. Since the tornado, he'd been driving her back and forth instead of letting her take the school bus.

"Oh, look, someone is working on the roof of the Old Town Hall." Lily pointed out her window as they turned onto Main Street. "Ms. Josie said people want it ready for Christmas. For Founders' Day. Ms. Josie said it will be a healing celebration."

"Ms. Josie obviously says a lot of things," Silas muttered, glancing in the direction Lily pointed. The sight of the half-finished building sent the same pang through him that he had felt when he first saw the destruction of the Old Town Hall. He and Kelly had been married there.

He pushed the memory back. Rebuilding the Old Town Hall seemed a waste of time. The old could never be replaced. It wouldn't be the same. All those memories were best left gone with the building when it was destroyed.

"What is Founders' Day?" Lily asked, suddenly animated. "Is that when people who lost things find them again? Like the place they set up for people who lost stuff after the tornado?"

Silas chuckled at her description. "No, honey. I heard it has something to do with the friendship of the two men who started this town, a Mr. Logan and a Mr. Garrison."

"Like Reverend Garrison? Who works at the church?"

"He's a relative."

"Reverend Garrison is a nice man." Lily sighed. "Alyssa always goes to church on Sunday to hear him preach. I wish we could go again."

Silas made no comment to that as he turned the truck in to the school parking lot. Since Kelly died, he had stayed away from church and God. Just keeping the boundaries marked off. God: up there and silent. Him: down here and busy. Never the two shall meet.

Silas parked the truck, pulled off his seat belt and turned off the truck.

"Don't get out of the truck yet, Daddy," Lily said, grabbing his arm.

Silas, his hand already on the handle, stopped, shooting his daughter a frown. "Why not?"

"I have something for you." She scooted across the seat and threw her arms around her father's neck. "Happy birthday, Daddy," she said, adding a noisy kiss. Then she gave him the bag she'd carried into the truck.

As he took the bag he felt a jolt of all-too-familiar guilt. She had remembered his birthday. Had planned for it.

He remembered how he had completely forgotten hers.

"Why, honey—" He swallowed down a surprising knot of pain. "Thank you. What is it?"

"You're supposed to open it and find out." Lily sat back with a self-satisfied grin.

Puzzled, Silas pulled out the package wrapped in a plastic grocery bag. When he unwrapped the framed picture, he did a double take.

Why had his daughter given him a picture of Josie Cane?

He masked his confusion and gave Lily a careful smile. "Thanks, honey. This is an interesting present."

"I got the picture from Alyssa for my birthday. And I think you need to have a picture of someone in your bedroom again. Like you used to have of Mommy."

The woman smiling back at Silas from the picture looked as if she was laughing at a secret joke, her long blond hair blowing away from her face. Her eyes held a hint of mischief, which made Silas think the stories about Josie's wild past held some truth.

"That's very nice. Thank you, Lily." He put the picture back in the bag, but didn't tell his daughter there was no way he was filling the spot that once held a picture of his beloved wife with a picture of this woman.

Lily sat back in her seat, her arms hugging her backpack, obviously not ready to leave yet. "Do you think she's pretty?"

"As pretty as she needs to be."

"I like Ms. Josie."

He gathered that. "I'm sure she's very nice."

"And she's a good teacher."

She gave him a sweet smile, which immediately made him suspicious. "I want to go to the after-school program again, Daddy. Can I? Please?"

Bingo. Silas heaved a sigh, marveling at her persistence. "We're not talking about that now, Lily."

Lily glanced over her shoulder again. "Can you please walk me to the school?"

Where did that come from? She was usually out the door and down the sidewalk before the truck rolled completely to a stop. Now she wanted him to walk her to the door?

"Of course." He got out, still puzzled.

The banging of hammers from various parts of town competed with the whine of saws as he walked around the truck to where Lily waited. Work was going on all over town, still repairing the damage from the tornado.

Thankfully the school had been spared the worst of the damage and classes hadn't been interrupted.

"Lily. Hi." A little girl's voice called out over the noise in the town just as Silas caught up with his daughter.

He turned and came face-to-face with a young girl holding the hand of the woman whose framed photo lay faceup on the seat of his truck. He shot a quick glance at his truck, wondering if Josie would have seen it as she walked past.

"Good morning, Mr. Marstow," Josie said.

"Ms. Cane."

Her smile wasn't nearly as friendly and open as the one in his picture and he was surprised at the touch of disappointment this created. But he tipped his hat all polite and gentlemanly, then smiled at Alyssa.

As he always was when he saw her, he was surprised how much Alyssa and Lily were alike. Same red hair. Same tip-tilted nose. Same slight build. Even Alyssa's sparkling green eyes held the same hint of mischief that Lily's could, which was probably why they were so close.

But the resemblance ended with their clothing. Where his daughter wore a faded Hannah Montana T-shirt, Alyssa wore a white button-up shirt so bright it hurt his eyes. Lily's pants had grass stains on the knees while Alyssa wore a cute, ruffled pink skirt and striped white, pink and green knee socks.

And Alyssa's shining red hair was done up in neat, fat braids tied with green-and-pink ribbons.

The girls looked like "before" and "after" pictures for laundry detergent.

"Did you start baking yet?" Lily asked, catching Ms. Josie by the hand. "'Cause I asked my dad if I could come to learn how to bake, and he said maybe."

"We would love to have you come back to the class," Josie said, shooting a puzzled glance his way.

He knew exactly what the question in her eyes was about. Once the phones were up and running in High Plains, he had called her and told her Lily wouldn't be attending the class anymore.

He had been diplomatic enough not to accuse her of carelessness, but she seemed to have drawn that conclusion. She had offered more apologies, but he was firm. He had said he wasn't going to compromise the safety of his daughter. Which made her mad. Which, in turn, made him mad.

They hadn't talked or seen each other since then.

"What are you making today?" Lily asked, swinging Ms. Josie's hand, her wide, happy smile creating a surprising spurt of jealousy in Silas. She never smiled like that at him.

"We're making cupcakes," Alyssa, holding Ms. Josie's other hand, put in.

"I want to learn how to make birthday cupcakes. For my dad. It's his birthday today, Ms. Josie."

"Is it, now?" Josie glanced back again at Silas. "Happy birthday, Mr. Marstow."

"Thank you, Ms. Cane," he said, stepping aside to let a group of laughing children slip past him.

"He's not very old yet, you know?" Lily said. "Do you think he's old?"

"I think he's exactly as old as he needs to be," Josie said, tilting her head to one side as she looked at him as if making sure.

"You sound like my dad," Lily said with a grin. "He said that you're as pretty as you need to be."

"Really?" Thankfully Josie didn't look at him.

"Do you want to come over to my house for a birthday party?" Lily asked. "Daddy, can we have a birthday party for you at our house? Can Ms. Josie and Alyssa come?"

A gust of wind picked up Josie's hair and tossed it away from her face and, as she smiled, she looked even prettier than her picture.

And for a moment he couldn't look away.

Silas yanked his attention back to his daughter, frustrated with the vague reaction Josie had created in him. He had no intention of going down that road again.

"We're not having a birthday party," Silas quickly added.

"I don't mind if she comes to the class," Josie put in. "There's enough room for her."

Silas thought of the work he had waiting at home and the convenience of working straight through until late afternoon before coming to get Lily.

He scratched his temple with his index finger, trying to decide. Lily would be over the moon and out of his hair, and he wouldn't have to feel guilty about her watching television all the time.

"When he does that scratching his head thing? That means he's thinking," Lily said to Alyssa.

Josie pressed her lips together, stifling a smile.

"I've got a lot to do," Silas said, feeling as if he needed to put up a bit more resistance. "I'm not sure it will work."

"If you're busy it would be a good thing that Lily comes," Alyssa said. "Then you can work all day."

Silas glanced from one girl to the other, feeling as if he was being played like a cheap guitar.

"I promise I'll take care of her." Josie's husky voice held a touching vulnerability. "I can't tell you how sorry I am that she and Alyssa got away from me that day of the tornado, and I realize you were frantic with worry, because so was I." Josie looked down at the girls. "And if these two promise to never do anything like that again, I'm sure we can believe them."

As she raised her brown eyes to his, bits and pieces of other conversations intruded. "Raising Cane," one of the guys at the feed store had called her, alluding to her wild past. A young man, apparently a onetime fellow classmate, followed this up with stories of some heavy-duty partying on Josie's part.

Silas didn't know any of the stories personally. He had moved here ten years ago from Colorado. Then he met Kelly, fell in love and got engaged. They were full of hopes, dreams and plans. Silas had dreamed Kansas was where it was going to happen for him and it had. He and Kelly started their life and those first few years he and Kelly had been too involved in their own plans to get caught up in the comings and goings in High Plains.

So all he knew about Josie Cane was that she had lived it up and partied hard until her sister died, leaving her with an orphaned niece.

Could he really trust this woman with his daughter?

"Please, Daddy. Please. I'll be so good." Lily ran up to him and grabbed his hand. "And I won't complain about watching television while you work or eating grilled-cheese sandwiches for supper every night."

Didn't that make her life sound completely pathetic compared to baking cupcakes with the lovely Ms. Josie? What else could he do but give in?

"If you could have her for today, that would help me out for now," he said.

"I promise to take good care of her," Josie said.

The ringing of the school bell broke into the morning. Josie bent over to give Alyssa a hug. "Have a good day, sweetie." Josie tweaked the ribbon on the little girl's braid, then stroked her cheek. "Love you."

"Love you, Auntie Josie."

"Bye, Daddy." Lily tossed off a wave, grabbed Alyssa's hand and the two of them ran off, Alyssa's perfect braids bouncing on her shoulders and Lily's crooked ponytail bobbing behind her.

The school doors fell shut behind the girls and Josie turned to him, pushing her hair back from her face. "Thanks for letting her come to the program," Josie said with a careful smile. "Alyssa has been after me for the past couple months to get Lily to come, but I knew how you felt about it."

"But they see each other every day at school."

Josie lifted her hand, then let it drop in a what-can-I-do gesture. "I don't understand the obsession with seeing each other every day, either, but I'm learning as I go."

Silas gave a short laugh. "I feel like every day there's something else I don't know."

"And just when you've got it, they throw something new at you."

Like a picture of their teacher.

"So I just let her come to the class? I don't have to do anything else?"

Josie shook her head, then glanced down.

Silas followed the direction of her gaze and saw her twist her wrist as she checked her watch.

Time to push off.

"Then I'll see you later today," he said, taking a step backward. "Gotta run."

"I promised my grandmother I'd be back right away,"

Josie added as if she felt the need to explain. "And I hope you have a happy birthday."

Silas thought once again about the birthday present lying on the seat of his truck.

And what was he supposed to do about that?

Chapter Two

"So what are you staring at?" Nicki's voice pulled Josie's attention away from Silas, who was getting into his truck.

"Nothing," Josie said with an airy tone, tucking her hair behind her ear in a casual gesture. She gave the toddler perched on Nicki's hip a gentle smile, hoping to distract her friend. "Hey, Kasey, how are you?"

Kasey blinked, then turned her face into Nicki's slender shoulder, her fingers tangling in Nicki's long blond hair.

"She's out of sorts today," Nicki said with a wistful smile. "She had a bad night."

Josie gently touched the toddler's wispy hair. "Nightmares, you think?"

"I wouldn't be surprised. I know I would have nightmares if I was found wandering alone on the riverbank, after a tornado had just swept through town." Nicki shuddered. "It still gives me the creeps to think how close she came to drowning."

"And still no word from her parents?"

Nicki shook her head, holding Kasey even closer. "Not since those people falsely claimed they knew her, hoping to cash in on the fund set up for her."

Josie shook her head. "I still can't believe people would do that."

The sound of a truck caught Josie's attention and as she glanced sidelong, she caught sight of Silas driving past. He was watching her. She flushed again and turned in time to see her friend give her a thoughtful nod.

"He's good-looking enough. In a broody sort of way," Nicki said with a teasing smile.

"Not my type," Josie said with a dismissive wave of her hand. Besides, he was a widower with a young daughter. Her life was complicated and messy enough.

She glanced at her watch. "I gotta run. My grandmother doesn't appreciate being left alone too long."

"How's she doing?" Nicki asked.

Josie waggled her hand. "Not great. She's still in a lot of pain."

"I'm sad for her, but at the same time, happy for me. Because the longer you stay here, the longer I have to convince you to change your mind about moving away."

Josie tried not to respond to the wistful tone in her friend's voice, but it was the plaintive look in her blue eyes that almost did her in. "I can't, Nicki. You know that no matter what I do, my grandmother won't let me forget who I was and what I used to do." She had struggled and prayed over her difficult decision to move. Since she had taken in Alyssa, her life had changed but it seemed her grandmother hadn't accepted that or forgotten Josie's part. And now, even worse, her grandmother was turning her disapproving eye on Alyssa, as well. "And it seems many of the people in this town are determined to remember, as well."

"How can you say that? Everyone in town thinks you're great. You help everywhere help is needed. Since the tornado, you've been working your fingers to the bone." She shifted Kasey to her other side, absently stroking the toddler's head with her cheek. "And that stuff you used to do—surely your grandmother can't still hold that against you?"

Josie sighed. "It seems she does. And if anything, having

her live with me has proved to me more and more the necessity of leaving."

"But Alyssa and Lily…" Nicki let the sentence trail off.

Josie fought her own guilt over Alyssa. She knew how close she and Lily were and how devastated her niece would be to leave her best friend behind, but it couldn't be helped.

Another quick glance at her watch showed her she had to move on.

"Sorry, Nicki. I really gotta run."

"Will you still cover my preschool class after lunch? I've got to take Kasey to the doctor."

"Absolutely. Drive safe."

"And I'm going to be praying something will happen to you to make you change your mind."

Josie just laughed. "It would take quite something for that to happen. See you."

Josie hurried down the street, glancing at her watch again, feeling a moment of guilt as she remembered doing the same in front of Silas. She couldn't help it. In the past month, time had become her nemesis.

After the tornado had left her and Alyssa's home uninhabitable, they had moved temporarily into one of the cottages belonging to the Waters family along the river.

And when her grandmother was discharged from the hospital, unable to take care of herself, unable to walk and also unable to move into her home, she had moved in with Josie and Alyssa.

Every day was spent caring for her grandmother and Alyssa, dealing with an insurance company who required endless reams of paperwork, making lists and appointments for her grandmother and trying not to grieve the loss of the things she had owned.

Josie hurried up the walk to the house. This morning the physiotherapist was coming for her grandmother, then she had promised Nicki that she would cover her preschool class after lunch.

Then she had to get what she needed for her own baking class later that afternoon.

As Josie ran up the temporary wheelchair ramp to the cottage, she heard her grandmother's shrill voice calling her name.

And she paused, her fingertips resting on the door.

Please, Lord, give me patience. Help me to care for my grandmother as I should. She waited a moment, as if waiting for a quick answer to that prayer to come raining down from Heaven, then she turned the knob and stepped into the cottage.

"I've been waiting for hours," Mrs. Carter called out as Josie walked down the narrow hall to her grandmother's room. "Where were you?"

Her grandmother lay on the bed, clutching the blankets, her frown indicating her displeasure with her granddaughter. The early-morning sun slanting in highlighted the frown lines puckering her grandmother's forehead and the lines of disapproval bracketing her pinched lips.

Betty Carter's long hair, her grandmother's pride, was already neatly brushed, waiting for Josie to put it up in the chignon Betty had worn from the day she was a bride.

"Alyssa wanted me to bring her to school today," Josie said, walking to the bed.

"Girl is up to something. You better keep an eye on her." Betty caught the bar that had been installed specially for her and eased herself to a sitting position. "I think she's headed for trouble. Just like you."

The stream of negativity made Josie wonder again why she hadn't listened to the doctor's suggestion to put her grandmother in a short-term care facility instead of trying to take care of Betty herself.

No one would have faulted her. Josie was trying to rebuild her life one piece at a time. She had the responsibility of her niece and she had her job and she had her plans. More than enough for one person.

But when Josie had found out her grandmother was being discharged early, she knew exactly why she had to take Betty into her own home instead.

Guilt. The eternal motivator.

Guilt over the fact that her grandmother had lain, in pain from a broken femur and shattered collarbone, for four hours after the tornado struck her home before rescue workers got to her. Guilt over not spending enough time with her grandmother when she was in the hospital. Guilt over a sketchy past Josie had tried to leave behind but one her grandmother would dredge up time and time again.

And threaded through this all was the slim hope that one day her grandmother would grant her scarce approval, turning to Josie with a smile instead of her habitual scowl.

"Alyssa is a good girl," Josie said quietly, defending her niece. "Just like her mother."

"You better hope she takes after Trisha—otherwise you'll have your hands full. Like I did. Visits from the cops. Phone calls from other parents. You were nothing like Trisha and even less like your mother. Debbie was a good daughter and a good mother. Good thing she didn't live to see what happened to her girls. One dead and the other nothing but trouble…."

Josie closed her ears to her grandmother's litany of shame as she helped Betty Carter to the edge of the bed, moving her just as the physiotherapist had shown her the last time she had come for a home visit.

"Just put your arm over my shoulder and we'll go up on the count of three. Ready?"

A few quick maneuvers had her grandmother in the wheelchair.

"My goodness, girl, could you be any rougher?" Betty frowned as she tried to get herself settled, pulling her pink, fleecy housecoat around her with one arm. "That collarbone will never heal if you aren't more careful and you made my leg hurt. Again."

"What would you like for breakfast, Gramma?" Josie ignored Betty's complaints as she shifted the wheelchair through the doorway. The temporary living arrangements had never been meant to be wheelchair accessible, but thankfully a volunteer who had come to High Plains to help with the rebuilding had built a rough ramp up to the front door.

"I'm not hungry." Betty closed her eyes and sighed. "You can do my hair right away."

"I'll need to get some elastics from my room first."

"Why didn't you think of that in the first place? I always have my hair done in the morning. You know that."

Josie walked to the room she shared with Alyssa, closed the door behind her and leaned against it.

"Please, Lord, give me patience," she whispered, clenching her hands into fists. "Please help me to love her as You love her."

She waited a moment, then pushed herself away from the door and walked to her dresser.

She shook her head when she saw the framed photograph sitting front and center on the dresser.

Her niece had come home from school one day with this picture of her best friend, insisting on putting it on the dresser.

In the picture, Lily held the reins of the horse and grinned at the camera, her hair brushed and braided. She wore a cowboy hat and blue jeans. Silas was on the horse, his mouth tilted in an unfamiliar smile. He wore a cowboy hat pushed back on his head and he leaned toward the camera, his arms resting on the pommel of the saddle, as if about to divulge some secret.

When Alyssa had brought the picture home she said it was so she could remember her friend when they weren't together in school.

Josie picked up the picture. Lily looked a couple of years younger than now, which made Josie suspect Lily's mother had snapped the picture. Hence Lily's neat hair. And Silas's warm smile that transformed a face that Josie had seen only scowling or frowning.

He wasn't a happy man, and she wondered what it would take to see that smile again.

She set the picture back on the dresser, snatched the elastics she needed out of a basket holding Alyssa's hair stuff and hurried back to her waiting and impatient grandmother.

"You took a long time," Betty said, scowling at her granddaughter.

As Josie brushed her grandmother's hair, she wondered what it would take to get a smile from Betty Carter, as well.

"Did you give your dad the picture?" Alyssa slipped her backpack on and tugged her braids loose from the straps. They always got caught. Sometimes she wanted to get her hair cut, but then she wouldn't look like her friend Lily anymore. Lily's dad would never let her cut her hair, so Alyssa kept her hair long, too.

Tommy Jacobs bumped her as he ran past them, heading out the door to catch the school bus. Alyssa was a bit angry with him, but then she remembered that he was a foster kid and he had lost his dog. When she thought about that, she felt sorry for him and wasn't mad anymore.

"Yeah. He looked kind of funny when I did, though." Lily dropped her books in her backpack, but didn't zip it up before she put it on.

"Like funny laughing or funny weird?"

Lily tugged on her hair and tightened her ponytail. "Funny weird."

Alyssa thought about this a moment. "Do you think that means he likes her?"

Lily shrugged as she grabbed her coat. "I asked him if he thought she was pretty and he said, 'She's as pretty as she needs to be.' I don't know what that means." She sighed. "Now what are we supposed to do?"

Alyssa bit her thumbnail while she thought. "Maybe just wait a day or two? Then we can try something else?"

"Maybe. But this matchmaking is taking a long time. I know my dad is lonely, because I see him looking sad when he's sitting on the porch drinking his coffee and I'm supposed to be sleeping. And I want a mom again. Like Josie."

"And I want a dad. But I don't know how to make getting them together go faster," Alyssa said, taking Lily's hand.

Auntie Josie was already at the church, so she and Lily walked down the street from the school. The town didn't look as messy as it had the day of the tornado, but the trees still looked sad. At least that's what Auntie Josie always said.

"I'm tired of waiting," Lily said as they turned onto Main Street. "And I'm tired of eating grilled-cheese sandwiches and hot dogs."

"My aunt makes good suppers. We had something called pesto with our pasta last night. I liked it, but Gramma said it had too much garlic. Gramma doesn't like much of the food Auntie Josie makes."

A truck drove past them with a bunch of wood in the back, and Alyssa's heart skipped. That looked like Lily's dad. Was he in town already to pick up Lily? Was their plan going to get wrecked already?

But the truck kept going down the street.

"Did you phone your dad and tell him the program is going an hour later today?" Alyssa asked.

"Yeah." Lily swung her jacket back and forth, the cuffs of her sleeves dragging over the ground. "Will we get into trouble for fibbing? Your aunt told him it was over at six."

Alyssa didn't want to think about that. "I don't think so. Because if your dad comes late, and he comes to my aunt's house to pick you up, maybe you both will eat supper with us. And that's good for our cause."

Lily brightened. "That would be cool. How will he know I'm at your aunt's place?"

"Aunt Josie will put a note on the door. Guaranteed."

"But would your auntie Josie invite him for supper?"

"You just have to say how hungry you are. And make sure you let my aunt know how good the food smells. Say something again about how you usually eat hot dogs for supper. She'll feel sorry for you for sure."

"Right. I forgot."

"And maybe you shouldn't drag your coat and make it so dirty. You don't want your dad to get mad about that."

Lily shrugged. "My dad doesn't care. I never get in trouble 'cause my clothes are dirty."

"Really? My aunt doesn't like it when I get dirty."

Lily giggled. "One time Daddy forgot to put soap in the washing machine and my shirt didn't get clean. I didn't tell him, 'cause I didn't want him to feel bad."

"Maybe Auntie Josie can give him some hints," Alyssa said.

"If our plan works, then maybe he won't have to do the laundry anymore."

"That would be so cool," Alyssa said with a grin.

Chapter Three

"He's not coming." Lily stood by the door, clutching the plate of cupcakes she had made for her father's birthday.

"He'll come, honey. Don't worry." Josie stroked Lily's hair, shooting an anxious glance down the street.

It was 6:36 p.m. The rest of the parents had come and gone, but no sign of Silas. A phone call to his home netted her a terse request to leave a message from the answering machine. So she did, but here she was, half an hour after class and still waiting.

Anxiety clawed at her. Her grandmother had been complaining all last week about how long she had to wait for supper. As it was, Josie couldn't leave her grandmother alone too long.

"Is Mr. Marstow coming?" Alyssa asked, her voice surprisingly perky in the circumstances. Josie was glad the children hadn't picked up on her worry.

What if something happened to him? As far as she knew he was all alone on his ranch.

Another quick glance at her watch: 6:37 p.m. She had to get going. Now. "Are you sure you don't know your dad's cell phone number?"

Lily furrowed her brow, her nose curling up at the same time. "I'm sorry. I forgot. I used to know it."

Josie thought for sure Silas would have drilled that information into his daughter's head.

"I'll write a note for your father and leave it on the door. I also left a message on his home phone. Stay right here and don't move one inch," she said, adding a stern note to her voice so the girls knew she was serious. "I'm getting some paper."

The girls were exactly where she had left them when she returned with the note. She pinned it to the door, hoping it would stay. "Okay. Let's go."

She slipped her purse over her shoulder and held her hand out to Alyssa.

"Lily wants to hold your hand, too," Alyssa said. "She doesn't have an aunt's hand to hold. Or a mother."

Josie glanced down at the mismatched clothes Lily was wearing and felt a touch of regret for the young girl. Though Josie had taken the liberty of brushing Lily's hair and fixing up her ponytail, it was obvious to Josie the little girl had chosen her own clothes.

"I can carry my cupcakes in my other hand," Lily said, shifting them and holding out her free hand.

Josie took it and smiled down at the young girl. "Then let's get going."

The walk along the river to their temporary home was quick. Thankfully the girls were willing to step up the pace and they got there in a few minutes.

"Is that you, Josie? What took you so long?" was the first thing Josie heard when she opened the back door to the cottage.

"Sorry, Gramma," she called out, dropping her briefcase on the floor and helping Lily set her cupcakes on the counter. "One of the parents hasn't come yet."

She hurried to the living room. Betty Carter was sitting in her wheelchair, looking out over the river, her hands clenched over each other in her lap. Josie paused when she caught a fleeting glimpse of sorrow in her grandmother's face.

What went on behind those sharp blue eyes? Did she have regrets? Did she miss all the people she had lost in her life?

Josie would probably never know. Her grandmother never opened up to her. Never showed anything that might be construed as weakness. And never told Josie that she loved her.

"I would have liked to know if you were coming," Betty said, the condemning tone in her voice sweeping away the moment. "A simple phone call would have been considerate."

Josie pressed back a reply. Her grandmother didn't like answering the phone, as she had often told her granddaughter. "I see Sally got you set up nicely," she said, her eyes skimming over the table beside her grandmother. A teapot, cup and plate of cookies sat within easy reach as did a book and a couple of magazines.

While Josie was at work, a few women from the church took turns stopping by to check on her grandmother. Sometimes they had to help her out of bed.

"That Fenton woman doesn't know the first thing about helping invalids. She jostled me so bad, my pain came back."

"Did you take the pills the doctor gave you?"

"They don't do anything." Betty flapped her hand in a gesture of dismissal. Then she straightened as Lily and Alyssa slipped past the doorway. "It's not polite to ignore your Gramma, you know," she called out with a sharp tone. "And who is that with you?"

Alyssa stopped, and Josie saw her give Lily an apologetic look. Then she turned and trudged into the living room, holding Lily's hand.

"Gramma, this is my friend Lily Marstow. Lily, this is my Great-Gramma."

"Pleased to meet you," Lily said.

"Is your dad Silas Marstow?" Betty turned her chair around to face the girl.

Lily nodded.

"Your mother died two years ago?"

"It makes me sad to talk about her," Lily said. "But someday I'll get a new mother."

Her assertion made Josie wonder if Silas had a girlfriend, which then made her wonder why she cared.

"If you'll excuse me, Gramma, I have to go make supper." Josie felt bad leaving Alyssa and Lily with her grandmother, but she had to start.

"We're going, too," Alyssa said, grabbing Lily by the hand.

"Don't you want to stay and talk to me?" Betty asked, sounding peeved.

"I want to show Lily my room before her dad comes." Alyssa beat a hasty retreat, giggling with Lily as they scurried down the hallway and into the room she shared with Josie.

Josie paused in the doorway, feeling a moment's sympathy for her grandmother. Betty had never been a pleasant person, and Josie was sure her injuries gave her a lot of pain. However, she didn't blame the girls for not wanting to spend more time with her. Betty was unfailingly critical. While her grandmother might have just cause to criticize Josie, given her wild past, Betty had no right to reproach Alyssa.

"Alyssa is turning out to be more and more like you all the time," Betty snapped.

"Alyssa is a good girl, Gramma."

"You better hope so" was Betty's only reply.

Josie sighed and returned to the kitchen, her brief moment of sympathy melting in the heat of her grandmother's glare and reinforcing, for Josie, the need to stick to her plan of leaving. That Betty disapproved of Josie was one thing, but to turn that disapproval to Alyssa, Josie couldn't allow. And she knew her grandmother wasn't going to change.

She got the rice cooking, made some more tea for her grandmother and was stir-frying the vegetables when a truck rumbled to a stop in front of the house.

Josie glanced sidelong out the window in time to see Silas Marstow come striding up the walk. Beneath the brim of his cowboy hat, she saw his face set in the same grim lines she had seen that day of the tornado.

Why did she feel a rush of guilt? It wasn't her fault he was late.

"Lily, your father is here," she called out, rinsing her hands and drying them off on her apron as she walked to the door. When she pulled it open, Silas stood on the step, one hand raised to knock on the door, the other on his hip, his eyes narrowed.

She had a feeling of déjà vu as his disapproval swirled around her.

"I thought this thing went until seven" were the first words out of his mouth.

Josie slowly shook her head. "No. I was sure I told you six."

Silas pushed his hat back on his head, scratching his chin with his forefinger. He hadn't shaved and his finger made a rasping noise against the stubble shadowing his jaw. "Lily told me seven. I wouldn't be so irresponsible as to leave my daughter waiting for an hour."

Josie bit back her next response, trying not to get baited by his anger. "You're here now. Come in, and I'll get Lily."

The cabin was an adequate size for Josie, her grandmother and niece, but as soon as Silas entered the kitchen, it seemed to shrink.

"Have a seat, I'll be right back," Josie said, pulling out one of the chairs she and Alyssa had managed to salvage from their home.

Lily and Alyssa were perched on Alyssa's bed when Josie entered the room.

"Your dad is here," Josie said again.

"Okay." Lily glanced at Alyssa who lifted her hands in a pushing motion, then Lily turned to Josie. "I like supper, you know."

Alyssa poked Lily and frowned.

Lily slapped her hand on her mouth. "Umm—I mean, I'm really hungry."

"Of course you are. It's supper time." Josie glanced from Lily to Alyssa trying to read the unspoken messages flashing between the two. Because, sure as kittens grow up, they were planning something.

"Let's go see your dad," Alyssa said, jumping off the bed and dragging Lily along behind her.

"Auntie Josie, can Lily and Mr. Marstow stay for supper?" Alyssa was asking as Josie entered the kitchen.

Josie was momentarily taken aback. Talk about putting her on the spot.

"I don't think we can," Silas said.

"But I'm so hungry," Lily said, glancing over her shoulder at Josie. "I don't think I can wait until I'm at the farm."

Josie hesitated, convinced Lily and Alyssa were up to something and not sure she wanted to be a part of it.

"Oh, don't be so rude, let the man and his little girl stay," Josie's grandmother put in.

Somehow Betty had worked her way to the kitchen and had decided to add her voice to the fray.

Josie felt torn between appearing to be rude and feeling as if she was being manipulated.

"You're welcome to stay, Mr. Marstow," she said, giving him a polite smile that let him know she didn't expect him to.

"Thank you, but I should get going." He read her perfectly.

"But I'm so hungry, Daddy. I can't wait." Lily tugged on Silas's hand, rubbing her stomach with her other hand.

Silas glanced from Josie to his daughter and she was convinced he was feeling as manipulated as she was.

"And it's your birthday," Lily added. "And I don't want to eat hot dogs again. Not for your birthday."

Now Josie felt like a real cad. Making the guy go home and make hot dogs for his birthday meal. "Please. Stay. I insist. We'll have more than enough."

"Auntie Josie always makes enough so we can have leftovers," Alyssa put in. "And we had leftovers yesterday even though Gramma doesn't like it."

Josie shot her a warning glance. Mr. Marstow didn't need to know the minutiae of their everyday life.

"Please, Daddy," Lily pleaded, sensing her father's weakening.

"Alyssa, why don't you and Lily set the table. Make sure you have five place settings put out," Josie said, putting an end to the awkward discussion. She gave Silas a cautious smile. "Now, you have to join us."

"And we have birthday cupcakes for dessert," Lily added.

"You come talk to me in the living room," Betty put in from the doorway. "I remember your wife."

And so, step by step, Silas and his daughter were pulled into the Cane family dinner.

As Josie directed the chattering girls, she put the finishing touches on supper. While she worked, her own emotions veered from annoyance with Alyssa and Lily for putting her on the spot and a curious sense of muted anticipation.

It had been six years since she had a man over for supper.

Six years since her responsibilities completely altered the course of her life.

Six years since she carried Alyssa away from the hospital, a little, confused girl of two, an orphan, with only her aunt to take care of her.

An aunt who, up until then, had lived life on her own terms and in her own way. Josie's life had taken a 180-degree turn and there were many times, since then, that she thanked God for a second chance to redeem herself. Both in His eyes and in the eyes of the community.

But she was determined to be a good mother to Alyssa, to focus solely on the little girl and her needs. As a result she seldom dated and, in the past three years, had only gone out a handful of times.

Now a man's voice reverberated from the living room, answering questions posed by Betty. A man was joining them for dinner.

"Tell Gramma and Mr. Marstow dinner is ready," Josie said, setting the pot of rice on the table. She glanced over the settings, a feeling of self-pity loomed. The extensive china collection, inherited from her sister, had been reduced to a few chipped plates, a couple of cups and four bowls she and Alyssa salvaged from her broken house under the watchful eyes of a crew who was sent to remove debris.

The plastic chairs hunched around the rickety table had been donated, scrounged from various households whose possessions were still intact and who had extra to spare.

Her dining room had once boasted an antique dining room set, also inherited from her sister, a hutch that her parents used to own and a living room set that Josie had saved up for dollar by precious dollar.

All gone, she thought with a pang of remorse as she straightened the faded tablecloth she had bought at a rummage sale put on by the town for the tornado victims. Sure she had the insurance money, but dollars could never replace what she had lost.

She pushed her emotions aside, struggling to count her blessings. She had Alyssa. She had her health. She had the enduring presence of God in her life.

And Gramma? a tiny voice questioned.

Well that was another ongoing story.

"We're here," Alyssa said, leading the mini procession into the kitchen with a grin of pride.

"Smells good," Silas said, pushing Betty's wheelchair into the kitchen. "Where do you want us to sit?"

Alyssa directed traffic and a few moments later, they were all settled around the table.

"Shall we pray?" As Josie glanced around the full table, a curious sense of well-being sprung up inside.

It felt good to see new faces around the table. And as Josie's eyes met Silas's, she felt the faintest hint of possibilities.

Which she immediately quashed as she bowed her head. She had her plans. They had only been put on hold until her grandmother was settled.

"Thank You, Lord, for food. For a roof over our heads. For the blessing of Your love," Josie prayed, "and thank You for the company that could join us this evening. May we be a blessing to each other. Amen."

Josie waited a moment, then looked up.

Directly across from her, Silas was looking past her, his mouth set in grim lines. As if he was disapproving of something.

Chapter Four

"**W**hat made you move here if you didn't know anyone?" Betty was asking, sounding unusually animated as she ate.

Maybe she should have supper company more often, Josie thought. Then she caught Alyssa pulling a face at Lily and she shot her niece a warning frown. Alyssa was getting positively giddy.

"I liked the size of the town. I liked the people I met," Silas said, seemingly unaware of his daughter's silly antics.

"And then you met Kelly, of course," Betty said with a coy smile. "Your wife was in the same Bible study I went to. She was a lovely, lovely person."

Silas gave Betty a tight smile but didn't answer.

"I remember the first time she came," Betty continued. "She wore a white dress. And the way she could quote Scripture. I'm sure her parents and grandparents were very, very proud of her, as were you," Betty said with a faint sniff.

The admiration in her grandmother's voice and the sidelong glance Betty shot her resurrected an unwelcome surge of self-pity. The underlying tone seemed to be that there were other children, grandchildren even, who could not create this pride. Who were unworthy.

Like Josie, for instance.

"Your wife was a treasure, Mr. Marstow," Betty continued. "A blessing from God."

"She was a treasure," Silas said.

Josie glanced at him as she caught the pain in his voice. But his attention was on the few pieces of rice he had left on his plate.

"Daddy said that God took our mommy away from us, so we don't talk about my mom or God," Lily put in. "But I miss her."

"I'm sure you do," Betty said, but her eyes were on Silas. She opened her mouth as if to say more when Josie interjected.

"Lily, why don't you get the cupcakes." Josie raised her voice just in case her grandmother decided to voice the words hovering on the edge of her usually sharp tongue. "I think most of us are ready for dessert."

"I'm not done," Betty said with a peevish voice as Lily and Alyssa jumped off their chairs and Josie cleared a space for the plate.

"I made strawberry ones." Lily set the plate with the assorted cupcakes on the table in front of her father. "But I didn't put pink icing on them, because I know you don't like pink."

Silas gave her a rueful little smile. "What color did you use?"

"Purple. With yellow flowers. Ms. Josie helped me make the leaves. She makes really, really nice leaves."

"We all have our talents," Josie said, with a light laugh. "Can I take your plate?"

"How long have you been doing this program?" Silas asked, glancing up at her as he handed her his dinner plate. Josie felt the faintest flutter as their gazes met.

She pulled her attention back to his question. "For the past six years. I took some childhood-development courses through a community college in Manhattan."

"And what made you decide to move back to High Plains?"

"Ms. Josie is a really good teacher," Lily said, not giving Josie a chance to answer, "I learned a lot today."

"That's good," Silas murmured.

Lily leaned forward, her hands folded in front of her on the table. "Can I please go again tomorrow? And tomorrow and all the time?"

Josie wanted to interrupt. Lily was really putting her father on the spot and she was sure he didn't appreciate it. But before she could say anything Alyssa cut in.

"My aunt Josie is very careful. All the time, she's very, very careful. And she would never let Lily run away like I made her do that day of the tornado." Alyssa's expression was so earnest it made Josie smile.

She glanced at the recipient of all this eagerness and caught a flicker of humor feathering across Silas's lips, as well.

And then his smile transformed his face. Laugh lines fanned around his eyes and a certain tension around his mouth faded away.

And Josie felt a tingle of awareness slip up her spine.

"I'll have to think about it."

"I would be really good," Lily put in. "And you wouldn't have to stop your work to pick me up."

Still smiling, Silas glanced at Josie. "It seems I'm getting ambushed."

"I would love to have her. It would be no trouble to add her to the roster."

"Okay. She can go."

"I'm done," Betty said, wiping her mouth with her paper napkin. "I can't swallow this dry rice."

"Would you like some more water?" Josie asked, reaching for the pitcher.

"No. I want to get out. I've been cooped up in here all day while you've been gallivanting around."

"We're having dessert right now," Josie said, struggling

to keep a patient tone in her voice as she cleared away her grandmother's plate.

"I don't want any. When you're done with supper, you can take me out."

"Can Lily and I take you for a walk, Gramma?" Alyssa put in, her face smeared with icing from her cupcake.

"I don't know if that's such a good idea," Josie said as she sat down.

She tried as much as possible to be the buffer between Alyssa and her grandmother's caustic comments. For the most part Josie was the direct target of Betty's ire, but lately Betty had been turning on Alyssa, as well.

Josie couldn't understand this. Alyssa was the daughter of Betty's favorite grandchild. Maybe it was because Josie was taking care of her. And not doing the job Betty thought she should. Maybe Betty thought Josie's younger behavior was rubbing off on Alyssa.

"We'll be real careful and we'll go slow." Alyssa popped the last bite of her cupcake in her mouth and wiped her fingers on her napkin.

"You've got icing on your face, missy" was Betty's frowning reply.

Alyssa obediently wiped it off, then glanced at Lily. "So do you." She giggled.

Lily wrinkled her nose, but ignored it as she took another bite.

"Hurry up, Lily," Alyssa said, wiping her mouth again. "We have to take my Gramma for a walk after Auntie Josie does devotions."

Lily gave Josie a puzzled frown as she licked her lips. "What's devotions?"

"We read the Bible and pray, dummy." Alyssa bopped Lily on the shoulder.

"Don't call her dummy," Betty snapped before Josie had a chance to reprimand her niece.

Josie bit back a comment, then walked to her bedroom for her Bible. When she picked up the brown, leather-bound book from her bedside table, she paused and smiled. This Bible was one of the few things she'd salvaged from her house. She had received it from Reverend Garrison after her sister's death. He had told her it would give her comfort.

And it had.

Reading the Bible had also given her the strength she needed to deal with her grandmother's anger when she found out Josie had been named Alyssa's guardian instead of her. The Bible was well thumbed and worn and one of the most precious things she owned.

Josie hurried back to the table and as she slipped into her chair, Silas frowned at the book she laid on the table.

Josie slid her fingers in the pages marked by the bookmark Alyssa had made for her. "We've been reading through the Psalms the past few weeks. Today we're reading Psalm 16," Josie explained as she opened the book.

She chanced another look at Silas who sat back in his chair, his arms crossed over his chest, his eyes narrowed. *Sheer defensive posture,* she thought.

Josie lowered her gaze as her mind cast back to Lily's innocent comment about God taking their mother away from them. Did Silas really believe that?

She hesitated, wondering if reading the Bible would bother him. But then she reminded herself of the comfort she had received from God's word. She began reading.

"'Keep me safe, O God, for in You I take refuge. I said to the Lord, 'You are my Lord; apart from You I have no good thing.''"

She didn't have to look up to sense Silas's antagonism pushing at her. But she read on, seeking God in the words. "'Lord, You have assigned me my portion and my cup; You have made my lot secure.'" As she read, she saw her grandmother fidgeting beside her, and Lily whispering to Alyssa who was looking down and grinning.

Was she the only one at this table who understood that they were reading God's holy word? She paused a moment, letting the words she was reading register both with her and the people sitting at her table. Then, she finished, "'...You will not abandon me to the grave, nor will You let Your Holy One see decay. You have made known to me the path of life; You will fill me with joy in Your presence, with eternal pleasures at Your right hand.'"

She smoothed her hand over the page, then carefully closed the Bible. "I know for me, those words give me great comfort. I know everyone here has faced some deep sorrow, but it is such a comfort to know we will see those we love again."

"Do you mean in Heaven?" Lily asked.

Josie shot her a smile, thankful she had heard what Josie had read. "Yes. I mean in Heaven."

Lily looked pensive, and Josie wanted to scurry to her side and sweep her into her arms. Alyssa was only two when her parents died. She barely remembered them but Lily obviously had memories of her mother. And she obviously missed her.

Then she caught Silas watching her, his mouth set in a harsh line of disapproval, a disconcerting contrast to the smile she had seen only a few moments ago.

"I can talk about her there, then," Lily said with a note of finality in her voice, her eyes fixed on Josie. "In Heaven."

Josie felt as if Silas was watching her, waiting for some slipup on her part. She assumed anything she might say to his daughter would be the wrong thing.

All she could do was smile at the lonely, hurting girl and hope that somehow, over time, she could show Lily how God could comfort her.

Then she lowered her head. "Let's pray," she mumbled.

But as she prayed, her mouth seemed to form one set of words and her mind another.

When the prayer was over, she looked up to catch Silas frowning at her, a peculiar expression on his face. She was about to ask him what was wrong when the ringing of the phone broke into the moment.

It was Reverend Garrison asking for her help.

"Sure. I don't mind," she said, picking up a pen. "I can start next week."

Josie chatted a bit more, getting some details and then hung up.

"What do you have to do now?" Alyssa asked as she started clearing the table.

"Reverend Garrison asked me to help make lunches for the volunteers working at the Old Town Hall," Josie said, scribbling a note on her already full calendar.

"I'm excited to see it finished," Alyssa said.

"I think it's cool," Lily said, her expression brightening. "My mom and dad got married in it. My mommy always said that was a happy day."

Silas was frowning. "That'll do, Lily."

"Sorry, Daddy. I forgot. What's past is past."

Her obvious parroting of a phrase she must have heard from her father created a deep melancholy in Josie. Why was he suppressing this? Surely this wasn't healthy?

Silas got to his feet, making a show of glancing at his watch, then he looked over at Josie. "Thanks for a delicious dinner. And thanks for the cupcakes."

"You should take the leftover cupcakes home," Josie said, holding up her hand to forestall him. "I'll put them in a container."

"That's fine," he said waving his hand. "We gotta go."

Lily shot an anguished glance at Alyssa. "But…but me and Alyssa are supposed to take Alyssa's Gramma for a walk. And you and Ms. Josie were supposed to—"

She got cut off when Alyssa grabbed her by the arm and shot her a warning glance.

Obviously something else was supposed to happen here.

"I'm sorry, Lily, but I have a lot to do at home." Silas's deep voice brooked no argument. "As I'm sure Ms. Cane does. Say goodbye and thanks, and then we'll be going. You'll see her tomorrow."

Lily gave Alyssa an apologetic glance, then slid out of her chair, gave her father her hand. "Thanks for supper, Ms. Josie. I had fun."

"Thanks for your hospitality," Silas said, giving Josie a tight smile.

"I'm glad you could join us." Josie got to her feet, still clutching her Bible.

"See you tomorrow," Lily said, waving goodbye to Alyssa, then she turned and trudged out the door behind her father.

"Are you sure you didn't get the paperwork? I know I sent in everything on your list." Josie pushed her hand through her hair as her eyes flitted over the letter she had just received in the mail from the insurance adjuster.

"I'm sorry, Ms. Cane, but we need the inspection certificate before we can proceed to the next step."

"I sent you the original."

"You didn't make a photocopy?"

On what, Josie wanted to ask. Her computer and the copier she used to own had long been relegated to a recycling depot. She hadn't had the funds to replace them yet because she needed the money from the insurance company, which she couldn't get until her paperwork was in order.

"Can you please check again?"

"I'll see what I can do, but you must understand this will delay your claim."

Of course.

"I understand." Josie forced a smile, hoping it balanced

the frustration creeping into her voice. She hung up, sighed once more and then the phone rang again.

Her grandmother's doctor. He wanted to set up a consultation with the orthopedic surgeon who had initially done the surgery on her femur.

"I'm glad to hear it," Josie said, pulling out her Day-Timer to schedule the appointment. "She still isn't walking and complains regularly about her collarbone." Complaining wasn't new for Betty, but the intensity of it had increased in the past few weeks.

"I agree that she should be further along in her healing process than she is," the doctor explained. "The plates look to be holding up well and other than the infection she fought, things have been proceeding the way they should."

"What is going on over there," Betty called out from her bedroom. "That minibus will be here soon and I don't want to keep him waiting like we always do."

Josie covered the mouthpiece of the phone with her hand. "Be right with you, Gramma." She turned her attention back to the doctor, flipping through her Day-Timer to find a day that worked for her.

Because of the extra work she had volunteered to do, most of her days were full, but she managed to squeeze out an afternoon to bring her grandmother to Manhattan.

"I bring my grandmother every day to the physiotherapist, I could possibly cancel one appointment to see this specialist."

They made firm plans for two weeks from tomorrow.

By the time she hung up the headache hovering at the back of her head had taken over with a vengeance.

She was just about to go to her grandmother when the phone ran again.

"Hello." She couldn't stop the curt tone of her voice.

"Sorry to bother you, Ms. Cane. This is Silas Marstow."

His deep voice created a tingle that eased away her curtness, but also invaded her insides in a most peculiar way.

"What can I do for you?"

"This is kind of awkward…." He paused, and Josie braced herself, wondering where he was going. "It's about Lily. If she's attending your after-school class, there's something you need to know. It's about her mother."

Here was her opportunity. It had been two days since Lily and Silas had dinner with her and she had been hoping to catch him alone, when he came to pick up his daughter, to talk to him about Lily's mother. But he always came and went so quickly, she never had the opportunity.

Until now. She took a deep breath, praying for the right words.

"What about Kelly?" Josie asked.

"I would appreciate it if you could avoid mentioning her mother at all."

"Do you think that's a good idea?" Josie asked, struggling to ignore the ringing of her grandmother's bell.

"That little girl cried for a month after her mother died. She didn't eat, she didn't sleep. Every time someone asked about…her mother…she grew hysterical. So, yes. I think it's best."

The ringing of her grandmother's bell grew even more insistent.

"I'm not sure it's wise, Mr. Marstow," she said, covering her one ear to drown out her grandmother's summons.

"It's the way it is, Miss Cane. And if you want Lily to stay in your program, then you'll respect my wishes."

The hard tone of his voice seemed to tell her there was no discussion. This was simply a statement of how he wanted things to be.

Though she wanted to dispute his stance, for now she had to respect it. Or run the risk of Lily not coming to the program anymore. Maybe once they got to know each other better, she could bring it up.

"I'll do that, Mr. Marstow," she said, struggling to keep her tone neutral. "Thank you for calling."

She heard a faint intake of his breath, as if he wanted to say more. Then she heard a click in her ear and the call was over.

Josie pulled a face at the handset. Wasn't he the hospitable one?

"Who was that on the phone?" Betty asked as Josie wheeled her out of the room. "You were yakking a long time."

"I was talking to the insurance adjuster about the house and Silas Marstow about his daughter."

"He's a good man, that Silas." Betty half turned, her eyes narrowing. "You seemed to be paying him a lot of attention when he was here the other day."

And why did that simple sentence make her feel suddenly self-conscious?

"He's the father of my student" was the only explanation she gave.

"He's a looker, that one. And his wife, nothing like you, my girl."

"The doctor called, as well," Josie said, hoping to sideline her grandmother's train of thought. "He was surprised you are still so immobile. He said according to the X-rays, you are healing quite nicely."

"Much he knows. Pain doesn't show up on X-rays, now, does it?" Betty spun around, her hands grasping the armrests of her wheelchair with a white-knuckled grip. "We just better not be late for that bus."

Five minutes later, Betty Carter was on her way to the hospital, and Josie was walking toward the animal shelter where she was helping Lexi whenever she had a spare minute. When she came back, she had to make some lunch for the men working on the Old Town Hall.

Thankfully that wasn't far away from the cottages, so she could leave her grandmother alone for a while so she could deliver the lunch. Betty would complain, but Josie wasn't going to let her grandmother's temperament keep her from helping the people who were rebuilding the town she loved so much.

Then why do you want to leave?

Josie pushed the annoying voice back into the nether regions of her mind. She didn't *want* to leave High Plains.

She *had* to. If she wanted to make sure Alyssa didn't grow up with the same disapproval Josie did, if she wanted to make sure Alyssa didn't walk the same path Josie had and live with the same, eternal regrets, they had to leave.

Chapter Five

"But I want to go to the clinic first." Lily sat back in the truck, her arms folded mutinously over her chest as the countryside flew by the window beside her.

"I told you, honey, we're not getting a puppy," Silas said as he eased his foot off the truck's accelerator. No need to speed and put both their lives at risk.

"But I still want to look at them."

"I have a bunch of other things to pick up before I get the medicine I need, Lily." Silas glanced at the list lying on the dusty seat between them. The vet clinic was the last stop on his list.

He had managed to finagle a lift of lumber from Garrison and he needed to make sure no one got it before he did so he needed to go there first.

"Do we have to go to that boring tool place again?"

Lily knew his routine well. It seemed every trip to town necessitated a quick trip to the hardware store for nails, screws or the odd tool he still needed to finish the cabins. "Unfortunately, yes."

Lily turned to him, her eyes bright. "If we go to the vet place first, you can leave me there while you do your other stuff then you can come back and pick up your medicine."

Silas blew out his breath, trying to understand his daughter's manipulations. "Dr. Harmon doesn't run a baby-sitting service."

"I'm not a baby. And Alyssa and Ms. Josie always—" Lily stopped suddenly.

"Always what?" he prompted, wondering what she would say about the friend she was forever talking about. Or her friend's guardian.

"Always…always tells me…that she… Dr. Harmon likes kids."

Silas fully understood that following him around was as interesting to her as watching the news on television. But though he felt sorry for her now, he knew he wouldn't after listening to an hour's worth of whining about how bored she was.

"I'm sorry, honey, but that's the way it is."

"I hate 'that's the way it is.' I hate it when you say that."

Silas didn't bother reprimanding her for using the word *hate*. Kelly hadn't tolerated Lily using a word that simply wasn't in his wife's vocabulary. But then, Kelly wasn't the one left behind with a grieving child and a tangle of seething emotions. What could she know about hate?

He heard a heavy sigh from Lily and one glance at the way her lips were pressed together told him he would pay for his stubbornness much longer than he wanted to.

So what was the problem with stopping at the clinic first? Nothing, really.

With his own sigh and a concession to his daughter, he made a right turn instead of a left and pulled up in front of the vet clinic. Before she got out of the truck, he caught her by the arm. "No dog. No cat. We're not walking out of there with any pet."

Lily's look was pure innocence. "Of course not, Daddy." Then she bounded out of the truck.

The familiar scent of medicine greeted him as his booted feet echoed in the quiet front of the clinic.

He heard the sound of muffled voices from the back, where Lexi kept the strays she had rescued, and caught Lily grinning at him like it was her birthday.

A figure appeared in the doorway, which made him look up. He felt a flicker of some forgotten emotion that disturbed even as it created anticipation.

"Can I help you?" Josie Cane stood in front of him, her blond hair pulled back, a blue smock covering her clothes.

"You're not the vet." As he blurted out his very suave response, out of the corner of his eye he caught Lily's sudden grin. He felt like smacking himself on the forehead. So this was the reason she wanted to come here first.

Josie waved a hand in the direction of the door she had just come through. "If you need some medicine, Lexi will be here in a minute. I thought…" Her sentence drifted off as a flush crept up her neck. "I'm just helping with the strays. Since the tornado Lexi's been running a bit behind on her work."

"You help here, you make lunch for the people working on the Old Town Hall." He shook his head and emitted a harsh laugh. "Where don't you work?"

He didn't mean for his comment to come out so condemning. It was just seeing her again that threw him off. Something about her made him feel both uncomfortable and at the same time created the faintest touch of yearning.

He couldn't go there, he reminded himself. He had to keep himself closed off. Secure. Safe.

But Josie just smiled. "This is my town, my community, and I want to pitch in where I can. And that's what you do when you…when you belong to a community."

He frowned.

"You don't seem convinced, Mr. Marstow."

"I'm not."

"Don't you think belonging and being involved in a community can help heal?"

It was her soft, deep voice that got to him. That and the way her eyes held his, as if she was digging deep into his soul.

Who did she think she was, giving him advice on healing? Why did she think it was any of her business when he had explicitly told her not to talk about Kelly?

"I think you're overstepping your bounds," he growled, unable to keep the words to himself. He felt a need to push her sympathy away, to blank out the sound of the sorrow in her voice. "You don't need to give advice on how to heal."

Josie straightened, and the faint smile hovering at the corner of her mouth faded away. "What do you mean?" Her voice held an edge that hadn't been there before.

"I'm not discussing this. Remember?"

Her eyes narrowed and she looked as if she wanted to say more, but wisely kept her mouth shut.

Lily cleared her throat, and Silas almost jumped. He had forgotten his daughter was still here. Thankfully he hadn't said anything truly foolish.

"I'll go see what's taking Lexi so long." Josie left, and a few seconds later, Lexi made an appearance. Her long, brown hair was pulled back, held by an elastic, and her white smock held a faint, reddish smudge.

"Sorry about that. Just got a frantic phone call from a pet owner," she said, flashing a dimpled smile at both Silas and Lily. "What can I do for you?"

"One of my bulls has been fighting an infection that won't clear up."

Lexi asked him a few more questions, then turned to the refrigerator behind her.

"Is Alyssa here?" Lily asked.

"Alyssa is in the back, feeding your dog," Lexi said over her shoulder as she pushed a box aside and pulled a couple of vials out.

"Her dog? What do you mean, her dog?" Surely Lily hadn't gone ahead in her quest to get a puppy.

Lexi set the vials on the counter and turned to her computer. "It's not her dog, per se," she muttered as she typed the information in, her attention on the screen. "But she was here a while back with Alyssa and they had this idea of adopting a dog as a present."

"Can I see him?" Lily asked, her voice taking on that gentle whine she had perfected and that he hadn't managed to find a way to ignore.

"If it's okay with your dad," Lexi said, glancing over at Silas. "He's just in the back."

It wasn't really okay. He had a bunch of things to do yet, but the look of yearning on his daughter's face was hard to ignore.

"Just for a few minutes," he warned.

Lily cheered and before he could tell her exactly how long she had, she had scooted around the counter and was gone.

"Did you want to see the dog?" Lexi asked as she pulled the invoice out of the computer.

"Oh, good trick," Silas said as he scribbled his signature on the bottom. "You know if I see my little girl playing with him I'm going to get all mushy, and she's going to turn her own puppy-dog eyes on me and I'm hooped."

Lexi laughed, and then the phone rang again.

"If you change your mind, I've got the strays just down the hall, to the right," she said as she picked up the phone and walked around the corner.

Silas was left alone. He glanced over the posters Lexi had hanging up. Checked out her bulletin board with its assorted advertisements and lost-and-found pets.

He saw a picture of a mutt-looking dog with a plea to 'plees help me find my friend, lost in the tornado,' signed by Tommy. Silas had heard about the little boy and couldn't help feeling sorry for him.

Silas glanced at his watch. Lily wasn't coming, so he had

no choice but to go get her. He didn't need Lexi's directions to find the dog. All he had to do was follow the sounds of voices.

He stopped in the doorway of a large room full of kennels stacked two high. Josie stood by one of the kennels, with her back to the door.

Lily and Alyssa sat on the floor, playing with a medium-size dog of indeterminate breeding. He was licking Lily's face as Lily was trying to hug him.

Once again Silas was confronted with the differences in the little girls. Alyssa wore a pair of pink shorts topped with a lace-trimmed shirt. Her hair was pulled back into a tight, neat ponytail tied with a matching pink ribbon.

Lily wore a faded denim skirt that had been too small last year and a sloppy, brown T-shirt that looked like its better days had happened when Silas was in school. From behind, Silas saw tangles in her hair that she hadn't reached with the brush this morning.

Why hadn't he noticed that? Josie was going to think he didn't care about his little girl.

"I love you," Lily was saying to the dog, managing to get her arms around him and squeezing him, disregarding the drool dripping down her shirt. "I wish you could come to my house. Then I would have someone to play with when I'm all by myself."

"When are you by yourself?" Alyssa asked, demurely stroking the dog's shiny fur.

"When my dad is busy," Lily said.

Josie, who was pouring water into a bowl for a cat in one of the kennels, glanced down at Lily. "What keeps your dad so busy?"

They hadn't seen him yet, and Silas knew he should make his presence known, but something made him wait so he could hear his daughter's response.

"Working on the ranch," was Lily's response. "He says he

has to keep busy or he'll go crazy. That's why he forgot my birthday. Because he's so busy."

Silas winced. He thought she had forgotten his lapse, but apparently not. And apparently her birthday was a big deal after all, even though she had repeatedly assured him it wasn't.

He had to do something about that.

And although "something" didn't include adopting a puppy, he wanted to make it up to her.

He quietly backed up a few steps, then coughed to warn them he was coming and walked through the doorway.

Lily kept her grip on the dog and granted him a gleaming smile.

"Isn't he a pretty dog, Daddy?" she asked, as she stroked the dog's fur. The dog turned his large brown eyes toward Silas as if seeking confirmation of the fact.

Silas glanced at the mutt with his patches of brown and black fur and begged to differ. "He's quite the dog," he said instead. "And no, you can't take him home."

Lily clamped her mouth shut, her face clouding over.

"He would keep Lily company," Alyssa added, as if her contribution to the discussion was all Silas needed to convince him. "When she's all alone."

They made her sound like she was an abandoned child when, in fact, she seldom wanted to come outside with him and preferred to stay in the house.

"She's got me," he said. "Lily, can you head out to the truck and wait for me there?"

Lily frowned, her attention on the dog between her and Alyssa. "Can't I stay here?"

"One...two..." Before he got to three Lily sighed and slowly pushed herself to her feet. She gave Alyssa a sad look. "See you on Monday," she said, heaved a sigh that resounded through the room, then left.

Silas glanced back over his shoulder, making sure Lily was indeed leaving the clinic, then turned back to Josie.

She was holding a kitten in one hand and nuzzling it with her nose. She smiled as the kitten rubbed its head against her face, then she looked up at Silas and her smile faded away. Why that bothered him, he wasn't sure.

He cleared his throat just as Alyssa got up and brushed the front of her shorts off. "I'm going to go keep Lily company," she announced, and marched off.

Which was perfect.

Silas waited another beat, then pushed his hat back on his head, wondering if he was doing something really dumb or if he was simply desperate.

Probably a bit of both.

He plunged ahead. "I was wondering if you could help me out sometime. Maybe next Saturday?"

Josie blew lightly on the kitten's ears, then looked up at him. "What do you want me to do?"

Silas scratched his forefinger on his temple, feeling decidedly awkward. "Well, you see, I forgot Lily's birthday."

"That was understandable. Wasn't that the day of the tornado?" Josie put the kitten back in the kennel and shut the door.

"Well, yeah. But that wasn't the reason I forgot." This was difficult and he wasn't sure where to go. "I want to get her something, but…"

"You're not sure what?" Josie offered.

"I know I don't want to get her that dog." Silas pointed at the animal Josie was putting back into another, larger kennel.

"Good call. Pets should be a family decision, especially where kids are involved." Josie closed the door and angled him a quick smile.

How about that? He did do the right thing once in a while.

"Did you want me to give you some ideas for a gift?" Josie prompted, walking to the sink in the room and washing her hands.

"I think I want to get her some new clothes," he said

suddenly. "But I don't have a clue about what she likes or what she should wear."

"And you want my advice?" Her voice held a note of incredulity.

"Maybe. If you don't mind."

Josie seemed to consider her reply as she dried her hands off. *Okay, this had been a dumb idea.*

"Actually, forget it. I'll get the salesclerks at the local store to help me."

Josie pursed her lips as if she was thinking. "I could make up a list for you. Some color suggestions, fashion choices."

Silas's head spun. He had never in his life gone shopping on his own for either Lily or Kelly. "Okay. But how would I know if it's right or not?"

Josie laughed. "I could meet you at the store, if you want. That might solve a lot of problems."

The idea of going on his own terrified him. But the idea of spending time with the beautiful woman before him might not be such a good idea.

Josie leveled him a glance that held a glint of humor. "You're allowed to ask for help once in a while, you know."

He was about to express his second thoughts when Lily and Alyssa came running into the back of the clinic.

"Look what we found," Alyssa called out.

She had her hand held out, a ring nestled in her palm. "Do you think it's the one that Reverend Garrison asked us to look for? The missing ring from the Logan family?"

Silas took the ring from her and turned it over in his hand. It was engraved with a swirling rose pattern barely legible through the dirt.

"Where did that ring come from?" Josie said, coming to stand beside him.

"It was under a pile of wood," Lily called out. "Can we keep it?"

"If it belongs to the Logan family, no. But I doubt that ring would have ended up all the way here in town. Can I see?" Josie asked, holding her hand out to Silas. He dropped the ring into her palm. She turned it over then shook her head. "It doesn't have a diamond, the way Reverend Garrison described the Logan ring. But it must belong to someone. Maybe there's an inscription inside."

Silas tried to read it but couldn't. "Here. You try."

"I don't see anything. Odd that it would just be lying by the clinic," Josie said.

"Can we keep it?" Alyssa asked.

"No," Josie and Silas said at the same time.

They caught each other's eye and shared a smile.

"Someone, somewhere is missing it, I'm sure," Josie said. "We should bring it to the lost and found at the church."

"But no one said they missed it," Lily said with a pout. "I think it's really pretty."

"Doesn't matter. Josie…Ms. Cane is right." Silas put in. "I'm sure if someone is missing this, they would like to have it back."

"I can return it," Josie said. "I'll be there tomorrow."

"Okay. That problem is solved, then."

But Josie held up the ring, staring at it, her expression suddenly melancholy.

"What's the matter?" Silas asked.

Josie started, then dropped the ring in her shirt pocket. "Nothing. It's just…my sister had a ring like this once."

"Could it be hers?"

Josie shook her head. "Highly doubtful. She was buried with it on."

Silas was surprised that she could speak so easily of her sister's death.

Then she flashed him a quick smile. "I'll make sure the ring gets brought to the lost and found."

Silas nodded and an awkward silence sprung up between them. He wanted to revisit his request for help with the birthday purchase for Lily but wasn't sure how to phrase it or even what to ask for. He didn't want to go into a clothing store on his own, but would Miss Cane be willing to come with him?

He was about to formulate his request when her cell phone rang. She gave him an apologetic smile as she flipped it open and turned away from him.

More volunteering, probably, Silas thought as he turned to leave. "Lily, let's go."

Lily glanced from him to Josie, then said a subdued goodbye to her friend.

Silas glanced back at the kennel, his eyes taking a momentary detour past Josie who still stood with her back to them. She was nodding her head.

Alyssa walked over to her side and leaned against her. Josie smoothed Alyssa's hair as she spoke, then slipped her arm around the little girl's shoulder in one fluid motion.

As he watched the easy interaction between Josie and her niece, weariness fell on his shoulders.

Josie made it look so easy. Like it was second nature caring for a little girl.

Each moment Silas was with Lily, he felt as if he was second-guessing each decision, each plan. And when he felt as if Lily was taking advantage of his wavering he overcompensated and got tough. Then he felt bad for laying down the law so unequivocally. It was a vicious circle. But how to get out of it?

"Let's go, honey," he said to his little girl.

The rest of his trip was surprisingly uneventful. Thankfully Lily didn't complain when he wouldn't let her listen to the radio at her usual million decibels or when he took a little longer at the feed supply or at the hardware store. She seemed more than content to either follow him around or wander off down aisles filled with "boring" stuff.

Her inexplicable amiability gave him a niggling sense of

unease, but then he accused himself of the usual second-guessing. He should be happy she was being so cooperative for a change.

It was on the tip of his tongue to tell her about his plans next week, but that would create a flurry of questions and excitement. He still wasn't sure what to do, so best leave things be for now, he figured as he headed out of town. He hadn't taken Josie up on her offer so he wasn't committed to anything.

Maybe he should just forget about it. Maybe he should just get Lily a dog.

And he was back to the beginning.

When his cell phone rang, he grabbed it, thankful for the diversion.

It was Adam. The buyer he had lined up for three purebred bulls. A minor purchase from a major cattle guy, but a potential foot in the door.

"So, those bulls, you putting them on your sale or can I still get them?" Adam asked as Silas turned the truck in to his driveway.

"They're yours if you take all three."

"If they throw the calves you say they do, then I'll be back for more next year."

Which would mean a much larger sale.

"I'd like them delivered a week from tomorrow. Sunday."

"I can arrange that. There's a local guy—"

"I want them delivered by you. Not contracted out to some guy who doesn't care in what shape they come to the farm."

Silas glanced at Lily who was swinging her feet, smiling at him.

Adam's ranch was an eight-hour drive. One way. There was no way he could take Lily along. She got carsick after an hour in any vehicle.

He'd delivered bulls before, but only short distances to

local ranchers. But Adam was exactly the kind of client he was trying to woo. And if Adam wanted his bulls delivered, Silas would find a way.

But what was he supposed to do with Lily?

A picture of Josie stroking Alyssa's hair flashed into his mind.

Silas dismissed the idea. He had a few other options. Sure, Lily had never stayed overnight anywhere for the past two years, but he'd figure something out. He had to if he wanted this sale and if he wanted to be fair to Lily.

"Okay. I'll get them to you next Sunday," Silas said. They chatted a bit more, then the conversation was over.

Silas snapped his cell phone shut and while it was still out, he called the neighbor lady who took care of Lily from time to time.

But she was gone this weekend and his backup plan, a high school senior whom he'd used once or twice, was also busy this weekend.

With a sigh he slipped his phone into the holder at his waist.

"Is something the matter, Daddy?" Lily asked as he pulled up to the house.

"No. Nothing's wrong. I just need to deliver some bulls and it will be a long drive for us," Silas said as he parked his truck in front of the house.

Lily's face drooped. "Can I please stay home?"

"I can't find someone to take care of you, punkin'."

"But I don't want to be sick again." Lily pressed her hand on her stomach, remembering the last time she'd come with him on a long trip.

Silas remembered all too well himself. Neither the attendant guilt nor the post-sick cleanup had sat well with him.

"I could stay at Alyssa's place," Lily suggested quietly.

Silas gave her a sidelong glance, his mind working over that possibility.

"I don't know, honey. We barely know her or Ms. Cane."

"I know Alyssa real good. And Ms. Josie told me that if I ever want to stay over, I can."

Silas wasn't surprised. Ms. Volunteer herself.

"You could bring me on Saturday," she said, turning to face him, as if sensing his hesitation. "Then you can leave early Sunday morning and be home at night and I won't miss you for too long."

Silas had to smile at his daughter's reasoning and how well she understood what needed to be done.

"And it would work because on Saturday morning you are going shopping with Ms. Josie and you can bring me to Alyssa's place. I can stay overnight and on Sunday you can bring your bulls away."

Silas shot her a frown. "I'm not going shopping with Ms. Cane."

"But I heard her say she would help you."

"When did you hear that?" Silas asked.

Lily turned her head away so fast Silas was surprised he didn't hear her neck snap.

"You were listening in, weren't you?" he insisted.

Lily wove her fingers together and stretched her hands out in front of her. "Maybe I heard a little bit about my birthday present."

And maybe she heard a lot.

"That would be nice to get a birthday present. And it would be really nice to stay overnight at Ms. Josie's. So I don't have to get sick in the truck," she added, dotting her *i*'s and crossing her *t*'s with a poignant sigh worthy of an Oscar.

He hadn't taken Josie up on the offer, but Lily's sigh hit his guilt buttons with deadly accuracy. He still wanted to get her a birthday present and he still needed a place for her to stay.

"I'll think about it" was all he said.

But when Lily was in bed and Silas was sure she was fast asleep, he picked up the phone. Put it down. Thought of his options, which were nil. Thought of the repercussions, which could simply be the result of overthinking.

Sure she was single. Sure she was attractive. But he wasn't looking. So he was safe.

He pulled in a long, slow breath, then dialed Josie Cane's number as he tried to kill two birds with one stone.

Chapter Six

"You look pretty, Auntie Josie," Alyssa said, looking up from the puzzle she was working on at the kitchen table. "I like it when you don't pull your hair back."

Josie put her hand up to her hair, wondering if she should have put it in her usual ponytail. Was she being too obvious?

And the lipstick? Should she have even bothered with makeup?

Should she have offered to help him buy some clothes for Lily? Shouldn't she have simply left him and Lily to Eileen and her limited inventory?

Josie stilled her spinning thoughts as she slipped a casserole in the oven and set the timer so the oven would go on while they were away. She was simply helping out a little girl.

And her very attractive father.

Her very complicated and frustrating father, she added as a reminder to herself.

As she rinsed off the dishes she'd used, she glanced out the window of the cottage. The window afforded her a view of Main Street so she would know if Silas was coming.

A truck drove into view and Josie's heart flipped, but it drove past. *Not Silas,* she thought, shaking her head at her silly reaction.

A knock at the door sent her heart pounding against her ribs. But it was only the babysitter, a high school student who lived down the road, recommended to her by Maya Logan, now Maya Garrison. Someone who Maya assured her could handle two rambunctious girls and one cantankerous grandmother.

While she was giving Carla, the babysitter, directions on what to do, Gramma rolled her wheelchair into the kitchen.

"And this is my grandmother, Betty Carter," Josie said to Carla, hoping, praying, her grandmother would be on her best behavior.

"Good afternoon, Mrs. Carter. Pleased to meet you." Carla flashed Betty a quick smile.

Josie's grandmother gave the girl a wary look. "You live down the street, don't you?"

"I do. Past the school. My father owns the restaurant on Fourth and Main."

"I used to eat at that place. Lovely food." Betty Carter's face softened and she smiled back at Carla. "I know your parents. Good people."

"Thank you."

Josie released her breath on a sigh of relief. Her grandmother had given her stamp of approval. All would be well while she was gone.

And yet, while Josie watched Carla and Gramma chat it up, she felt a sliver of pain. Why was her grandmother so easy with other people and so judgmental with her?

Sure she'd made mistakes, but didn't six years of caring for her niece and Betty balance the books?

Josie's thoughts were interrupted by the growling sound of a diesel truck pulling up to the house.

She ran to the window just as Silas stepped out of his truck, wearing his habitual blue jeans. He walked around the truck, then helped his daughter out. Today Lily looked a little more presentable, but the denim pants she wore barely reached her ankles and the sweater sleeves hung well above Lily's slender wrists.

Helping Silas get her some new clothes was a good idea, she rationalized.

But as they walked up to the house, Josie noticed Silas hadn't taken a suitcase for Lily. Had he changed his mind about Lily staying overnight? They had both decided not to tell the girls, to spare each of them the excitement this news would create.

Just before they reached the ramp, Silas glanced at the house, his eyes zeroing in on her.

Josie pulled back from the window, her face heating up. She looked like some silly teenager waiting for a date. She pressed her lips together, second-guessing the linen pants she had chosen and the coral sweater. Too dressy for a simple shopping trip. She should have stuck to blue jeans, a T-shirt and jean jacket.

Then he was knocking on the door and Alyssa was running to open it.

This was followed by another flurry of introductions and instructions and an exchange of cell phone numbers between her, Silas and the babysitter.

"Now, make sure you call if you need anything, Carla," Josie said as she grabbed her purse. "I'll keep my cell phone on."

She glanced at Silas, but still he said nothing about the overnight visit. He must have changed his mind. Good thing she didn't say anything to Alyssa.

They said their goodbyes then Josie was following Silas down the wheelchair ramp to his truck. A light breeze tossed her hair around her face, making a few strands stick to her lipstick.

As she brushed them away, she saw Silas opening the passenger door of the truck then holding out his hand to help her in.

Her gaze grazed his hand and for a moment she was unsure whether she was supposed to actually take it or whether she even should.

"Who said chivalry was dead," she joked as she ignored his hand and lifted her foot to step into the truck.

But she had underestimated how high his truck was and as she lost her balance, he caught her by the elbow. She struggled a moment, still trying to get in on her own, but gravity won out and she fell sideways.

Her cheeks grew even redder as her shoulder came into contact with his chest, his hand still holding her arm. "I'm sorry," she muttered, trying to regain her balance. "I didn't think I needed any help."

"A common mistake," he said with a dry tone, as he gave her a quick, ungainly push and then she was sitting on the seat.

He slammed the door and as he walked around the front of the truck, Josie took a deep, slow breath, forcing herself to relax.

Just a shopping trip, she told herself. *You're just helping out a single dad for the sake of Lily. It's all about Lily. Relax, would you?*

But when Silas got into the truck, she shot him a quick sidelong glance, surprised to see him doing the same with her.

"I noticed you didn't bring a suitcase for Lily. Did you change your mind about having her stay?"

"No. I didn't."

Josie waited for him to elaborate but he said nothing.

"Do you have an idea of where you want to go?" she asked.

"I was hoping you would navigate. I know nothing about shopping." He shot her a quizzical glance. "As you well know."

"In that case turn right when you leave here and we'll head toward Manhattan."

Silas frowned. "That's a half hour away."

Josie nodded. "I know, but there's a lovely store there that I've shopped at from time to time for clothes for Alyssa. Eileen Struthers, who owns our local clothing store, doesn't have a lot of selection yet. But when we come back, we can go to her for shoes and a few other things."

"Okay. You know best." Silas turned the truck engine on and country music blasted out of the truck's radio. His hand flew to the knob as he cut off a singer midtwang. "Sorry. I let Lily pick the volume and the station. Not my usual fare."

"What do you usually listen to?"

Silas dropped his arm across the back of the seat, his hand a few inches from her shoulder. He half turned in his seat to look behind him, his other hand spinning the steering wheel as he negotiated a backward turn.

Josie relaxed when his hand returned to the steering wheel.

"I like it quiet when I'm driving," he finally replied when he was driving back down Main Street. "What about you? What do you usually listen to?"

"I don't admit this to many people around here, but I like jazz if I'm in the right mood. Folk music. Classical. Bluegrass if the sun is shining and I'm driving out in the country and I'm in need of a banjo fix."

Silas flashed her a puzzled look. "Bluegrass?"

"Of course. It's good ol' mountain music. Part of our heritage."

Silas's frown morphed into a half smile. "Not Kansas's heritage."

"There's not many songs about farmers and wheat fields," Josie countered. "So I'll pilfer what culture I can from the Southern states."

His smile shifted but he didn't reply and the silence that Silas preferred filled the cab.

Josie sat back, content to watch the town slip past the

window. This end of High Plains hadn't been hit as hard as where she lived and they drove beneath a canopy of trees whose changing leaves created a blaze of color missing from her neighborhood.

"I miss this," she said, unable to keep the wistful tone out of her voice. "The trees in our neighborhood are just stumps and empty branches."

"When can you move back into your house?" Silas asked.

"I don't know."

"Why not? I noticed the other houses in town seem to be coming along."

"I'm having paperwork issues with my insurance company." Josie let a sigh slip past her lips. Thankfully it was Saturday, so she had a break from the endless phone calls and paperwork required to get things back in order. And as an extra bonus, the excuse of helping Lily gave her a valid reason for a break away from her grandmother and away from Alyssa. "But I'm thankful I have a place to stay for now."

"And your grandmother's place?"

"It will be ready in a couple of weeks, but she isn't doing well, so I doubt she'll be moving back home soon." Which reminded Josie, she had to tell her grandmother about the appointment she had set up. Betty wouldn't be happy. She hated going to the physiotherapist's, claiming she didn't do her any good and she hated, even more, going to see any doctor. Claimed they knew nothing.

Put that aside. Right now you're away from the house and you should have taken this break a lot sooner.

The houses of the town thinned out and soon they were in the country. Most of the fields had been combined and worked up already. Some tractors were pulling seed drills, planting fall rye and spring wheat.

And so the cycle continues, Josie thought, wondering where she would be come spring. Would she still be stuck in

High Plains? Caring for Betty in the tiny cottage that was only supposed to be temporary? She couldn't think about that. She had a plan. It was only on hold for a while, that's all.

"How badly was her house damaged?" Silas's question broke into her thoughts.

"Not hugely, but I don't know when she's moving back. So, for now, she's my responsibility."

"I think it's admirable that you are willing to take care of your grandmother," Silas said after a few miles of silence.

"Don't give me too much credit, I just do what I have to. Josie Cane, volunteering again." The words came out in a rush before she could stop them. Josie blamed her lapse on her circling thoughts. "Sorry. You didn't need to hear that."

Silas kept his gaze ahead as the power lines flipped past them. "I'm going to make a wild guess based on the one evening I spent with you and figure you have your troubles with her."

Josie pressed her lips together, as if to keep back the thoughts she suppressed every day.

"You are allowed to admit to a few failings, you know," Silas said.

His voice had taken on a lightly teasing tone that was at odds with his usually broody expression.

"I've got more than a few, as you probably well know. I'm sure you've heard the stories of my wild past."

Silas shot her a quick glance and nodded. "I heard them and, to tell the truth, when Lily and Alyssa took off from the church the day of the tornado, your reputation affected my decision to pull Lily out of the program."

Josie swallowed down a beat of disappointment.

"But I was wrong. I shouldn't have let your past get in the way of your present." He gave her a careful smile that seemed to settle into the lonely places of her heart. "It's past and I'm sorry. You're a caring person and it shows. I know I can trust you with my girl."

He glanced at the road, then back at her, his smile growing broader. Warmer. His words of approval making a home in her heart.

Josie couldn't look away and for the merest heartbeat possibilities beckoned. They were both single. And she was lonely.

She cut off that thought, and cut off the connection. She couldn't start anything with him. It wouldn't be fair to him or her. And besides, his life was way too complicated for her.

"Thanks for that," she said quietly. "I appreciate it."

"So, you were born here? In High Plains?" Silas asked, continuing the conversation.

"Lived here all my life. My parents were born here."

"So you must have a lot of family here?"

Josie shook her head. "My grandparents moved here when my father was little. He was their only child."

"Must have been hard for your grandmother and you when your parents died."

Josie shot him a frown. "You know that?"

He shrugged her question aside. "Small town. I know a few things about you."

"I know she was very sad," Josie continued, preferring to ignore the latter comment. "I think it was also difficult for her, raising me and my sister. I wasn't the easiest granddaughter."

"But you're taking care of her now."

"Only until she can be on her own. Then I hope to move away."

"To where?"

"I had plans to move to Ohio in August. I have a friend who lives there. I did have a job lined up…until the tornado. But I'm sure I'll find something else."

"Is Alyssa okay with that? I mean, she and Lily seem to be pretty close."

"Alyssa doesn't like it at all. But I'm doing this for her as well as me."

"What do you mean?"

"It's complicated. But it's for the best. I have to get away from here as soon as I can." Josie stopped herself there. Silas didn't need to know about her struggle with her grandmother and Josie's fears for Alyssa.

She turned back to the view, preferring to focus on the surroundings she was presently in instead of a past that hung over her like a dark cloud and an uncertain future.

Thankfully Silas took the hint and instead turned on the radio. Josie let the songs about someone else's heartache, problems and tears distract her from her own life.

A few songs and muttered directions later, Silas was parking his truck in front of a large clothing store. He got out of the truck and paused, one foot on the curb, the other on the street, as if hesitating.

Josie joined him on the sidewalk. "Is there a problem?" she asked.

"This place has all women's clothing," he said in a flat tone.

Josie caught the faintest downturn of his mouth, the narrowing of his eyes and it made her smile.

"Be careful, Silas," she said as she slipped her purse over her shoulder. "Here be dragons."

"Dragons I could handle," he said. "It's all that potpourri and candles and other stuff that gets to me."

Josie laughed and patted his arm. "I'll be your guide."

He drew a breath and stepped up onto the sidewalk. "Thank goodness. I'd never go to a place like this by myself."

Josie laughed again, and pushed open the door, not even bothering to see if Silas was following. There were just some things he had to do on his own.

But she heard him right behind her.

She strode confidently past the dreaded candles and cards directly to the children's section at the back of the store.

She stopped at a rack of shirts and pants and looked up at

Silas who was still glancing around, as if any minute pot-pourri might come raining down on him.

"We need to establish how much you want to spend and what you are looking for," she said.

Silas pulled his attention back to her and blew out his breath. "What do you think she needs?"

Everything, Josie thought.

"Why don't you start with something basic," Josie suggested instead. "A couple of shirts and a pair of pants. She doesn't strike me as a dress kind of girl."

"You got that right. The last dress she wore was the one that..." His voice faded away and he pressed his lips together as if holding back what was going to come out. "Anyway, she hated it. I think she cut it up."

Josie suspected he had unwittingly stumbled onto the no-man's-land of memories of his wife. Memories he seemed bound and determined to banish.

She turned to the rack in front of her. "If you want her to look a bit more feminine, you might like a skirt instead. Something in denim. Not frilly but yet cute. Put a pair of striped tights with it and I think you'd have a hit."

"Sure."

"What do you think of this shirt?" She held up a yellow T-shirt with long sleeves and an orange-and-blue crocheted flower on one side. "A vest on top and you'd have an outfit for her birthday present."

Silas glanced around and shoved his hand through his hair in a gesture of defeat. "Yeah. Whatever."

He wasn't being cooperative, but Josie was nothing if not persistent.

She led him to another rack and showed him a few more items she thought were cute. All of which garnered her the same listless response.

She was trying to keep her frustration with him down. Sure, men didn't like shopping, but this was supposed to be his birthday present for his daughter. She thought he would show more enthusiasm.

Ten minutes later, Josie dropped another shirt's hanger on the metal rack with a clang.

"Am I doing something wrong, Mr. Marstow?"

He pulled his attention back to her. "No. No. It's all good."

"I haven't gotten a very enthusiastic response from you for your own daughter's birthday present."

Silas narrowed his eyes again and a hint of fear whispered over her skin. His dark, level eyebrows, when lowered, created an ominous, threatening look.

But Josie tried not to be intimidated and pressed on. "I thought you wanted me to help you with this," Josie said. "If this doesn't matter, we can go home."

Silas gave no reply, and Josie stifled her own frustration. "Maybe we should go." She was about to leave, when she felt a hand on her shoulder. She turned to Silas, raising her own brows in question.

Silas pursed his lips and blew out his breath. "Truth is, Miss Cane, I don't have a clue. That's why I asked you to come. You asked me back at your house if Lily was still staying overnight. You noticed that I didn't take a suitcase. I couldn't find one and I didn't want to take her clothes in a paper bag. And the other truth is, I didn't even bother taking her clothes because I think they're all too small. Or worn out, or out of date, or whatever it is they're not supposed to be and are." He raised his hand in a gesture of defeat. "So that's where you come in, okay?"

His long confession was enough to soften Josie's heart, but she caved when she caught the fleeting glimpse of vulnerability passing over his face.

"Essentially we need to give her a whole new wardrobe," she said.

"Essentially. Yes. And essentially, I don't have a clue what a new wardrobe should look like."

Josie nodded slowly. "Then the next question is, how much do you want to spend?"

"I don't have unlimited funds, but whatever it takes."

"It's a good thing you specify the lack of unlimited funds. Because to tell a woman to spend whatever it takes is a recipe for a high credit-card bill." Josie flashed him a smile to show she was kidding and to lighten the suddenly heavy atmosphere. "So, let the games begin."

She walked over to the sales rack. "Not the best time to shop for winter clothes, but we could buy some summer shirts and layer them. She's the same size as Alyssa, so..."

Josie flipped through the clothes and pulled a couple of shirts off the rack. Then, making a quick decision, handed them to Silas. "If you want me to make all the decisions, you get to be the Sherpa."

With a good-natured shrug, he took the hangers and for the next half hour followed her around the store. Josie would have liked him to make some choices, but she had never shopped with a man before, so wasn't sure what to expect.

"This one has a button missing, so we can probably get a discount," Josie mused, holding up a shirt. "I could sew one on at home. And these jeans have a stain. One laundering and it'd be gone."

"Why don't we get the ones without a stain," Silas offered. "I'm not a laundry pro."

"It's not her size." Josie held up a jacket and frowned. "What do you think of this one?"

"Looks good."

Josie lowered the coat, and gave him a careful smile. "I realize that you want to defer to my judgment, but you haven't expressed an opinion about anything I've picked so far."

Silas raised his hand, palm up, in a gesture of defeat. "You seem to know what you're doing. I already told you I don't have a clue."

"But she's your daughter and it's your present and you're the one who has to look at her. You must have some preferences."

Silas heaved a sigh as he clutched the clothes she had already chosen, but Josie didn't back down.

"I don't like blue on her," he said finally.

"Okay." Josie hung the coat back up. "What do you like?"

"I like green."

Josie plucked the green coat from the rack. "Green it is." She handed it to him. "I don't imagine you ever went shopping with Kelly."

The silence that fell between them at her casual comment was so heavy it almost hurt her ears.

And Josie realized she had said the *K* word.

She felt like she should apologize, then stopped herself. Talking about Kelly was normal and healthy.

She wished she felt confident enough to throw out another casual question about his wife, but then a quick sidelong glance nipped that idea in the bud.

His eyes were narrowed again and his lips pressed together so tightly, she thought they might break.

Not today, she reasoned.

"We need pajamas yet," she said in her best cheery-teacher voice. And she strode away not bothering to see if he followed her. She found a frilly, long nightgown with a ruffle on the bottom. "How about this one?" she asked, holding it up for his inspection.

He frowned and shook his head. "No. She'll hate it. She's not a ruffles-and-lace girl."

Josie didn't want to push her taste too hard on Silas, but she was pretty sure, in this instance, he was wrong.

"Not for her everyday clothes, no. But I think, in some ways, she's a closet romantic. And a nightgown is a great way to express that."

Silas's frown deepened and Josie took a chance and laid the

nightgown on the pile of clothes, ignoring his faint cry of protest.

Fifteen minutes later Silas was swiping his debit card through the machine and smiling at the sales clerk when she commented on how happy one young lady was going to be.

"Your wife has great taste," the clerk added as she handed a number of the rustling plastic bags to Silas.

Josie didn't bother to correct her as she took the rest of the bags. The girl would be embarrassed and who knew how Silas would react.

She walked out of the store, waiting as Silas unlocked her door. This time she allowed him to help her into the truck.

Questions, comments, advice all hovered, waiting to be voiced. She knew he had given his reasons for not talking about his wife and if she knew him better, she would bring it up. As it was, she kept her comments to herself.

The radio filled the silence until they reached the welcome to High Plains sign.

"What's next on the agenda?" Silas asked, his tone of voice making Josie wonder if she had imagined that clench of anger back in Manhattan.

"If you have time, I'd like to pick up a few things for her at Eileen's. Underwear if she needs it. Socks and hair ties."

"Why didn't we get that at the store we were just at?"

"I like to support our local businesses when and where I can. I would have gone to Eileen's for clothes, but she's still stocking up and her selection is still limited."

"Does she carry suitcases?"

"You're thinking for Lily?"

"I'd like to give her some of her clothes. For staying at your place tonight. And I don't want her to carry them in a plastic bag."

Josie smiled at the firm note in his voice. "I'm sure we can find something there." She gave him directions and once again they were entering an all-female domain.

At least Eileen didn't have the potpourri Silas abhorred.

"Hey, Josie. How's it going?" An overweight young woman, about Josie's age, ambled over toward them, her buttons valiantly struggling to keep the fronts of her blazer together. The part in her blond hair was a dark streak, evidence of her actual hair color. "You still going a mile a minute volunteering all over the community?"

"Keeping myself out of trouble, Eileen," Josie said, glancing around the store.

"That's a switch for you," Eileen said with a giggle as she shot Silas a knowing glance.

"Looks like you're slowly getting your stock together," Josie said, choosing to ignore Eileen's not-so-subtle comment, as she glanced around the half-full store. Only a couple of mannequins graced the floor, displaying some of Eileen's wares. One of them was missing a nose, the other one three fingers on the left hand.

"Oh, it's coming. My suppliers are so slow. I'm just glad I got my store up and running as quick as I did, and thanks again for the help. I might need you in a week or two. I'll finally be getting my new shipment in." Eileen shot Silas another glance as she twirled a lock of blond hair over her finger. "What can I get for you today?"

Josie glanced at Silas who lifted his shoulders in a shrug, so she told Eileen what they needed and the woman waddled off, humming as she went.

Josie caught Silas staring at the disfigured mannequins.

"Those mannequins have always looked like that," Josie said, pointing to the redheaded figure with the nose missing.

"Oh. I thought maybe..."

"The tornado? Nope. Eileen inherited them from her mother who used to run this store. Can't bear to part with them. Says they're like family."

"My family is suddenly starting to look pretty good."

Which brought up another question. "Where is your family, by the way?"

"I've got a sister who lives in California. My parents are in Florida. Absence makes the heart grow fonder."

And Kelly's family?

The question hovered but Josie didn't give it shape. Silas might see it as intrusive and for the past while they'd been getting along quite well.

A faint electronic beeping from the door announced another customer.

"Well, Josie Cane," a voice called out as Josie turned. "How is your grandmother doing?"

The woman speaking was elderly, short and stooped. Her tiny face was framed by a shock of bright red hair that hung longer on one side of her face than the other.

Trudy Anselm's wig was crooked again, but Josie didn't think she'd appreciate having that fact pointed out in public. Her purple velour jogging suit was a hopeful touch, as were the blindingly white running shoes. Josie had never seen Mrs. Anselm, her grandmother's neighbor, poking along faster than a leisurely amble.

"My grandmother is doing okay, Mrs. Anselm." Josie didn't bother to elaborate. Trudy Anselm probably knew more than Josie did.

Trudy's bright blue eyes flicked from Josie to Silas and a knowing smile slipped over her face. "Well, Silas, nice to see you come out of your shell." She poked a bony finger at Josie. "But you want to watch yourself with this girl. Don't let those soulful eyes fool you. Underneath that innocent expression, she's a pistol."

"I'm helping Mr. Marstow pick out a birthday present for his daughter," Josie said to let Trudy know exactly which way that particular wind was blowing. Trudy Anselm may walk slowly, but her pace was steady and it wouldn't take long for her to waft false gossip through the town.

Mrs. Anselm's eager expression faded, and Josie assumed the message had come through.

"I miss you coming over. Haven't had decent cookies since you and your grandmother moved into those Waters cottages. Tell your grandmother I said hello and that I'm praying she'll get over all that trouble she's having getting walking again."

"The physiotherapist is hopeful that she'll be walking soon," Josie said.

"Tell her I'll stop by on Monday again." Trudy's button eyes shot from Josie to Silas. "So just shopping?"

"Just shopping," Josie assured her.

"Probably just as well," Trudy said.

Josie gave her a wry smile, wishing Trudy didn't know so much about her past. Of course her grandmother had kept her good friend posted about Josie's wild comings and goings when she was younger.

But at the same time, Trudy made it sound like Josie was still carrying on the way she had when she was much younger and infinitely more foolish.

Having Silas hear that bothered her more than she wanted to admit.

"Here we are," Eileen chirped. She spread her findings on the counter. "Socks. Underwear. Hair ties and some barrettes. I also found some cute tights that had come in with the last shipment. And here is a bag you could use for a suitcase. I have a few others if you're interested but this looked like something a little girl would want. This is just an idea. If you see something else—"

"This all looks good." Silas didn't even confer with Josie as he pulled out his wallet. "I'll take it all."

"But don't you want—"

"It's fine." He handed her his credit card and shifted his feet while he waited for the transaction to be processed.

Josie suspected his sudden impatience was a result of

shopping overload and guessed the shoes weren't getting purchased today.

He grabbed the bags as soon as Eileen handed him the receipt. Josie had to scurry to keep up with him. As he opened the truck door, she paused, holding his gaze.

"Is everything okay, Silas?" She gave him a careful smile as her mind ticked back over their conversation. She couldn't remember saying anything that might have made him angry.

His eyes held her gaze and his scowl eased away. "Yeah. I suppose."

He looked as if he was about to say something, then changed his mind. He closed the door, walked around the truck, then got in.

As he started the truck, Josie sorted through the bags. "Do you want to give her the whole works at once, or should I just pull out what I'll need for the weekend?"

Silas rested his hands on the steering wheel, looking ahead as his thumb tapped out a quick rhythm.

"Silas?" she prompted, as she packed up the pajamas they had just bought.

He glanced back at her again. "Umm…are you sure you're okay with having Lily stay overnight?"

"Completely sure." But even as she replied, she picked up on a vague sense of unease. Probably ignited by what he'd heard the past half hour. "Are you okay with it?"

Silas kept his eyes straight ahead. Then he sighed. "Of course I am."

Josie waited for him to elaborate on what was bothering him, but he said nothing more as he put the truck into gear and pulled out of the parking spot. So she made her choices from the clothes they had purchased, pulling the tags off and slipping them into one of the other bags. "Did you take any toiletries for her?"

"Behind the seat."

"Then we'll take them out at the house." Josie zipped up

the bag and set it on the floor, wondering what was going through his mind.

"You seem to be quite the busy little bee, helping out as much as you do?" he asked. "Is there any place you don't help out?"

Josie shifted her brain around, trying to keep up to the sudden switch. "I do what I can, though there's much more that needs to be done."

"Why do you bother?"

"This is a small town that has been dealt a huge blow. It's part of my responsibility to pitch in and to help."

"In spite of how people talk to you? How they bring up your past?" Silas's voice grew hard as he pulled up in front of the cottage.

Josie felt as if reluctant gears were switching into place. His sudden silence after Eileen's comments. Click. The way he looked when Trudy was talking. Click. Other comments he had made. Click. He had said, previously, that he trusted her, but surely what the people in the town said must give him second thoughts.

"Lily is perfectly safe with me," she said quietly. "I'm not the person I used to be."

"Sorry. No. I didn't mean…" He pulled the keys out of the ignition but didn't get out of the truck yet.

"I mean, I'm not surprised if you have doubts." She added a light laugh to show him that she understood. "There are people in High Plains who've left town to avoid being reminded regularly of their failings. A foul in an important basketball game. The time they put their parents' car in the ditch. The costuming mishap in the church play." Josie shrugged. "My misdeeds have been legendary and considering everything I've done, on the whole people are pretty easy with me."

Silas turned to face her, his arm across the bench, his hand a finger's width away from her shoulder. "I told you before, I trust you with Lily, Josie. I wouldn't have asked if I didn't."

He held her gaze a beat longer and Josie couldn't look away. A slender wisp of a forgotten emotion whispered through her mind as their eyes held.

She swallowed and forced her gaze away. *Don't start. Don't go there. Too complicated, too problematic.*

Her eyes landed on the wheelchair ramp and she was reminded once again of the most important reason she couldn't allow herself one moment of attraction to Silas.

She had to leave High Plains. In spite of her declaration to Silas that she wanted to help people in this town, she also knew that if she stayed, her grandmother would suck her and Alyssa dry.

Chapter Seven

"This is the best present ever." Lily's eyes danced over the pile of clothes surrounding her. Then she launched herself at Silas and grabbed him awkwardly around the neck. "Thank you, Daddy. Thank you so much! You picked exactly the right clothes."

Silas glanced at Josie over his daughter's shoulder. She gave him a thumbs-up, pleased to see him smiling.

"Ms. Cane helped me," Silas said, patting her awkwardly on the back.

"You spent way too much of Silas's money," Betty Carter grumbled from her corner of the small living room.

"I'm not that easily influenced, Mrs. Carter." Silas gave Lily another pat on the back, then got up from his chair. "Sorry to rush things, but I have to get up early tomorrow morning."

Josie nodded and got to her feet, as well. "Lily, why don't you say goodbye to your dad and then you and Alyssa can get ready for bed."

"Goodnight, Daddy" was all Lily said. She was about to leave, when she caught Josie's eye.

"You might want to kiss him goodbye," Josie said. "You won't see him for a while."

"Oh, yeah." Lily scurried back and then stopped in front of Silas as if not sure of what to do next.

Thankfully Silas bent over, kissed her on the cheek then gave her another pat on her head. "See you in a couple of days," he said.

As Lily spun away, Josie felt a momentary pang for the awkwardness of the exchange. She thought back to that moment when Silas had dinner with them and he had watched as Alyssa crawled onto her lap. He had glanced at Lily, his expression holding a mixture of melancholy and puzzlement. As if he wasn't sure himself if he should do the same and how to go about it.

"I better be pushing off," Silas said, grabbing his jacket from the back of the chair.

Josie walked him to the back door and just before he opened it, he turned to her. "Thanks again for all your help. I know I bugged you about all the volunteering you do in town, but I'm grateful you decided to do a bit more."

"It truly was my pleasure," she said warmly.

Silas tilted her a quizzical smile, and she felt a moment's mortification. Surely he didn't think…

She caught herself. It *had* been her pleasure. She had fun doing it. *Don't read more into your own comment than you originally meant,* she reminded herself.

"If you need to get hold of me." He pulled a card out of his wallet. "This has my cell phone number on it. I'll have it on most of the time."

Josie glanced down at the card. "Bar M Ranch?"

"That's my brand."

"I'm guessing the *M* is for Marstow," she said as she looked for a space for the card on the bulletin board she had hung up by the phone.

Silas glanced at the board, and for a moment she saw it through his eyes. Notes about phone calls she had to return and appointments she had to meet were layered over each other.

And in large, angry letters, tacked to the middle of the board, a note to call the contractor. Again. And the insurance company. Again.

"Busy lady" was all he said.

Josie didn't deign to answer him as she tacked the card on the bulletin board.

"I'm guessing that's about your house?" he asked, gesturing to her note.

"Paperwork isn't my forte."

"Yeah. Hardly seems fair, does it. The paperwork on your end involves writing the insurance company a check once a year, yet when you want something from them, they need stacks of forms."

"And I seem to forget which form I'm supposed to send when. And I always seem to forget to make the copies they like so much." She gave him another quick smile. "But I imagine you want to get going."

"Thanks again," he said, lowering his voice. "For taking care of her and for all your help today."

"Lily seemed happy."

"She was thrilled." Silas slipped his hat on his head and sighed. "I didn't think clothes mattered so much to her."

Josie caught a note of concern in his voice. "I'm sure it doesn't usually. And she would have been content to keep wearing what she had," she said, trying to reassure him.

"I don't think I started paying attention until she started hanging around with Alyssa. Your niece is always so neatly dressed and her hair always looks cute." Silas shrugged. "I don't know if I'll ever get the hang of doing Lily's hair."

"Lily can learn to do it herself. If you want, I can teach her a few basics."

Silas's gaze caught and held hers. "Helping again, Ms. Cane?"

"It's what I do, Mr. Marstow."

He gave a soft chuckle. "I better be going. I'll call you when I'm on the road."

"I should be around most of the time."

Their brief interchange, his promise to call as they stood by the back door drew a picture out of Josie's past.

Her own parents, saying goodbye to each other as her father left for work. Conversation by the back door, lingering goodbyes.

The shorthand of a married couple. *I'll call you. I'll be here.*

I'll miss you.

A band of longing wound itself around Josie's heart. Longing for the give and take of a relationship. The expectations and the promise to fulfill them.

Then, when his eyes caught hers, for the briefest of moments awareness arced between them, as if he'd been thinking the same thing.

A hint of a smile crawled across his lips, then he turned and was gone.

Josie waited a moment, watching as his truck reversed out of the driveway, unwilling to break the fragile moment.

"Josie. What are you doing?"

Reality intervened in the form of her grandmother, and Josie was pulled back to her own obligations.

She supervised the girls' teeth brushing, then brought them to her bedroom. While Lily was checking out yet another part of her birthday present, Josie had set up a foam mattress on the floor and put a sleeping bag on it. Now the two girls were arguing over who was going to sleep where.

"But I'm the guest. I'm supposed to sleep on the floor," Lily said, dropping onto the mattress, hugging a book she had pulled out of her backpack.

"That's why you're supposed to sleep on the bed, silly," Alyssa said with a giggle. "Because you're the guest."

While Josie was pleased to see her niece practicing the

generosity she had hoped rubbed off, it was time for the girls to settle down.

"Why don't I pick a number between one and ten and whoever guesses it gets to pick where they are going to sleep," Josie said.

"I guess two," Alyssa said.

"I guess seven," Lily replied.

"It's seven," Josie said. "How did you guess that?"

Lily slipped into the sleeping bag she sat on. "My mommy always guessed that number, too...."

"Josie is just like your mommy," Alyssa crowed. "That's cool."

Josie wondered how cool Silas would think that was. Perfect Kelly and Raising Cane. Hardly a comparison.

"Okay, let's say your prayers," Josie said, perching on the edge of Alyssa's bed.

"Just like my mommy, again." Lily just beamed. "My mommy always said prayers with me, too. When she wasn't too sick."

"What prayer did she say?" Josie asked.

"I can't remember it all, but it was a song that said something about a tender shepherd."

"The same prayer as we sing," Alyssa said with a note of awe in her voice. She looked at Josie, her eyes wide with amazement. "Did you hear that, Josie? You always say the same prayer as Lily's mom."

"It's a well-known song," Josie said, passing off their comparisons as mere coincidence. "Let's start, shall we?"

She went through the song with the girls, watching as Lily tried to sing along. She only knew a few of the words. Josie was pretty sure Silas didn't sing the song with her, or maybe even bother with evening prayers.

The thought disturbed her, because it seemed that Kelly had.

When they were finished, Lily lay back, still clutching her book. From here it looked like a photo album. "That was really nice." Lily's smile trembled a moment. "I remembered my mommy for a while."

Her comment tore at Josie's heart and she bent over and gave the little girl a hug. "I hope you don't mind remembering your mother," she said quietly, stroking Lily's hair away from her face.

Lily shook her head, slowly, but Josie saw the faint glisten of tears in her eyes. "Do you know any stories about my mommy?" she asked.

Josie hated to break her heart but she had to shake her head. "Sorry, honey. I might have met her, but I didn't know her."

"Your Gramma knew her."

"Your mom went to Bible study with my grandmother."

Lily sighed. "I miss her, but I like to remember her."

Josie brushed a kiss over her forehead. "I'm sure she would want you to remember her," she said quietly, hoping her comment didn't violate Silas's policy.

"I'm glad I could stay overnight," Lily whispered. "I like you, Miss Cane."

"I like you, too." Josie gave her another kiss, then wrapped the blanket extra tight around her. "I hope you have good dreams in this bed."

She tucked Alyssa in and kissed her and as she left the room, gave them a warning about talking too long.

But as she turned off the light, she knew her warning had been forgotten in the space of the time it took for the door to shut behind her.

No matter. Tomorrow was Sunday. They could sleep in for a while. She just hoped the girls had settled down by the time she went to bed.

"How do you think we're doing?" Alyssa whispered after Josie left.

Lily sat up and wrapped her arms around her knees. "Your aunt and my dad were talking a long time."

Alyssa sighed. "I thought maybe he would kiss her goodnight." She and Lily had been watching around the corner, but nothing had happened.

Lily shook her head. "My daddy doesn't believe in kissing on the first date. He says kisses are for the most serious part."

"How do you know that?"

Lily didn't say anything for a minute. Then she sighed. "I heard my mommy teasing him. Just before she died. She asked him that when he went on dates again, would he stick to his rule. About kissing on the first date. He didn't say anything, but he looked mad."

"Anyway, what they did today wasn't a date," Alyssa said, slipping out of bed. She walked to the door, pulled it carefully open, then shut it again. She ran back to her bed and hopped in. "She's still busy."

"Okay, maybe it wasn't a date, like going to the movies and stuff, but they were by themselves for a whole afternoon. What do we do?"

Alyssa pulled a box out from under her bed. "Now we move on to the next part of the plan."

Two hours later, after balancing the checkbook, playing a game of cribbage with her grandmother and getting Betty settled for the night, Josie slipped into the bedroom again.

She left the door open while she changed into her nightgown and in the crack of light that came into the room, she saw Lily's photo album lying on the floor beside her bed.

She bent over and as she picked it up, she caught a glimpse of the picture on the front of the album.

She guessed the beautiful redheaded woman was Kelly Marstow. She was glancing over her shoulder, holding a baby in her arms. Lily, Josie guessed.

Her hair flowed in a long waterfall of auburn curls down her back, the sun catching reddish highlights in it, her face and a sprinkling of freckles and her deep brown eyes held a hint of promise. Her mouth was curved in an elusive Mona Lisa smile.

Her vibrant beauty made Josie feel drab and insipid.

Although why that should bother her, she didn't want to consider.

But as she put the album on the dresser behind Lily, a deeper, sadder emotion took hold of Josie. Lily missed her mother and, Josie believed, she missed talking about her and reliving the memories. She thought of Silas's phone call warning her not to talk about Kelly with Lily. And she wondered how much Silas missed his wife.

After struggling to read her Bible in the light coming from the hallway, she said a prayer for Lily.

And for Silas.

"I'm excited to go to church," Lily said. She did a twirl around the kitchen then stopped, smoothing her hand over her new skirt. "And I'm excited about my new clothes. Do I look nice?"

"You shouldn't be so vain," Betty snapped, clutching her mug of tea. "God doesn't look at your clothes. He looks at your heart."

"But it is good to show respect for God by putting on our best clothes," Josie said, countering her grandmother's criticism as she finished washing the breakfast dishes.

Josie didn't bother admonishing her grandmother for speaking so harshly to the young girl. Lily didn't seem bothered by it and Josie knew any reprimand she gave Betty was a waste of breath.

Josie wished she knew why her grandmother grew more harsh and bitter with each passing week. Maybe it was the pain she had to endure, maybe it was sharing a home with her and Alyssa that was wearing her down.

But the trouble was Betty's constant carping and fault finding was starting to wear her down, too.

"I like my new clothes," Lily said, facing Betty straight on, her hands on her hips in a defiant gesture. "And I think God likes them, too."

Alyssa, drying the dishes, threw a horrified glance at Josie, as if expecting, any minute, lightning to strike her friend.

Josie was surprised, as well, at the little girl's temerity. But she wasn't sure she should reprimand her. Lily hadn't done anything wrong and Betty had a sharp enough mouth. If she thought the girl was out of line, she could take care of it.

But Josie got her next surprise. Betty simply spun her wheelchair around, heading toward the porch door.

"I think we should get going," Josie said. She wiped her hands and ran to the bathroom. She only had time to run a brush through her hair and swipe a bit of lipstick over her lips.

That would have to do, she thought, pulling a face at her reflection.

An image of Kelly Marstow flashed into her mind. In comparison, Josie's eyes looked pale and her hair limp.

Josie spun away and grabbed her corduroy blazer from her bedroom. Comparing herself to Silas's wife was futile. She'd never match up in many, many ways.

"Isn't the sun warm today," Lily said as she skipped ahead of Josie, Betty and Alyssa. She spread her arms and spun in another circle. "C'mon, Alyssa, come and spin with me."

"You'll ruin your hairstyle, missy," Betty said.

Lily kept skipping, once again ignoring Betty's comment. Alyssa glanced over at her great-grandmother, then let go of Josie's hand and joined her friend.

By the time they got into the church, Lily and Alyssa were happier than when they left the house and Betty crankier.

Josie greeted the people at the door, then took the bulletin and rolled her grandmother to their usual spot. Josie settled the giggling girls into the pew beside her, gave them a warning glance and picked up the bulletin.

"Another fundraiser?" Betty grumbled. She shifted in her wheelchair, shooting an annoyed glare at Alyssa and Lily. "I didn't sleep good at all. That Alyssa was giggling all night."

Thankfully the organist started playing the first song and Josie didn't have to listen to anymore of her grandmother's complaints. Betty would never, ever even think of speaking during the worship service.

Josie sang along, her spirit refreshed by the words of the songs and the singing of the congregation. Though she tried to spend time in daily devotions, coming to church filled a deeper need for connection with God's people. In the days following the tornado, many people seemed to feel the same. People who, in the past, had never attended were now coming more often.

Though Josie wanted to feel positive about the sudden surge in attendance, she was also realistic. She knew that people, in times of difficulty, often turned to God. She had done the same after her sister and brother-in-law died.

But thanks to Alyssa, Josie had realized she needed, for the sake of her niece, to make a regular commitment. And because of that commitment she knew she had to trust God to help her in all the relationships in her life.

Including dealing with her grandmother.

Josie glanced sidelong at Betty, once again trying to understand her grandmother. Trying to figure out what it would take to win a word of approval from her. To see approbation in her eyes instead of condemnation. It would be wonderful to make peace with her before she and Alyssa left for another state.

Reverend Garrison announced the Bible reading and Josie pulled the Bible out of the pew, thankful for the distraction. Ever since her grandmother moved in with her, Josie had become hyperaware of Betty's criticism and carping. The only positive was she was that much more determined to take her and Alyssa away from it all.

"Philippians 3, starting at verse 12," Reverend Garrison read. "'Not that I have already obtained all this, or have already been made perfect, but I press on to take hold of that for which Christ Jesus took hold of me. Brothers, I do not consider myself yet to have taken hold of it. But one thing I do: Forgetting what is behind and straining toward what is ahead.'"

Reverend Garrison read further on, but the last sentence caught Josie's attention. *Forgetting what is behind.*

Josie felt a touch of melancholy. Forgetting what lies behind wasn't easy in a small town. Her mind slipped back to her shopping trip with Silas and his comment about people bringing up her past.

She still wasn't sure what to make of his reaction. Whether he was bothered by the stories or whether he was bothered by the fact that they were still being circulated.

Probably the first, Josie thought, returning to Reverend Garrison who was now closing the Bible. She was eager to hear what he would have to say about the passage. To find out if she could gain some comfort from it.

Lily started fidgeting and Betty shot her an angry glare but Lily wasn't the least bit fazed by her. Alyssa leaned over and pulled Josie's head down. "Lily has to go to the bathroom," she whispered.

Thankfully they were sitting closer to the back. When they came back Lily sat down, but she played with the children's bulletin, dropped her pencil, twirled her hair and in general had a hard time sitting still.

"Make that girl behave," Betty hissed at Josie after a few minutes of this.

What could she do? Lily obviously wasn't used to being in church.

When Alyssa and Lily started whispering together, Josie

sat between them. By the time the service was over, she was tired and a bit cranky herself. She needed her time of worship and encouragement and exhortation. Her time to refuel for the work of the week.

Instead she'd been refereeing two rowdy girls and one out-of-sorts grandmother.

Thankfully the sun was still shining when they got out of church. The girls were still full of high spirits, which they obviously needed to get out of their system.

"Let's go have a look at the Old Town Hall," Josie said, forcing a note of brightness into her voice as she pushed Betty down the ramp. "That will be fun."

"I want my cup of coffee," Betty grumbled, twisting her fingers together on her lap.

"You'll get it later," Josie assured her, keeping her smile intact. "I thought we could all see how the work is progressing."

"Yay. Let's go," Lily called out, grabbing Alyssa's hand.

Josie didn't bother reprimanding them or telling them to slow down. They wouldn't have heard it.

"You've got to keep that girl under control better than you do, Josie Cane. She's going to turn out exactly like you."

Forgetting what lies behind.

The words mocked Josie as she pushed her grandmother toward the house. And how was she supposed to forget when she was reminded daily, if not hourly of the many and varied ways she had messed up in the past.

"I sure hope they get it done by Christmas, in time for Founders' Day," Josie said, looking up at the structure. The new wood gleamed in the fall sunshine, but much needed to be done yet. The problem was volunteer fatigue.

The last time she had brought lunch for the volunteers, only two people had been working. The other two men didn't show up that day.

The need was still so great. Josie's gaze flitted past the

half-finished structure to the town beyond. Houses were being rebuilt and every day the sound of hammers rang through the town. Everywhere except her house. Thanks to the delay with the insurance company, nothing had happened there for the past two weeks.

"My mom and dad were married here," Lily said, breaking into Josie's pity party.

"Are you sure?" Josie asked.

"I have a picture. My mommy looked so pretty," Lily said with a wistful note. Then she glanced at Josie, guilt etched on her features. "Though I'm not supposed to talk about her."

Josie thought of the album that Lily carried around and knew Silas was wrong to keep the memories so tightly stored away.

"What kind of flowers did she have?" Josie asked.

Lily brightened. "They were orange and white and so was my mommy's dress."

"Your mom's dress was orange and white?" Alyssa asked, scrunching up her face in an uncomprehending frown.

"No, silly. The dress was white and it went way out in the back and it was all lace with short sleeves."

Alyssa sighed, her eyes taking on the dreamy look that young girls adopt when thinking of brides. "That sounds so pretty."

"My dad had a brown coat and pants on and he looked really handsome. He never wears the suit anymore."

Josie tried to imagine Silas in a suit, but all she could conjure was a tall man wearing scuffed cowboy boots, blue jeans frayed at the hem, a twill shirt and five o'clock shadow.

A much more appealing picture.

Josie shook the image and the reaction free. This was Lily's father she was thinking about, she reminded herself. The man clearly still hung up on his dead wife.

"Can we go inside?" Lily asked.

"I don't think it will be that safe." Josie steeled herself at the flash of disappointment on Lily's face. "But we can look in one of the windows."

Josie struggled to navigate the work site with her grandmother's wheelchair, ignoring Betty's complaints and protests.

Lily and Alyssa were looking in the first window they found, cupping their hands around their face so they could see better.

"Do you think that's where my mom and dad were standing when they got married?" Lily asked.

Josie left Betty behind as she joined Lily at the sawdust-speckled glass.

"Looks to me like they would have gotten married over there," she said, leaning closer and pointing to the front of the building.

Lily didn't say anything, but sighed gently, her breath disturbing the dust that had settled on the window. "I bet it was a beautiful wedding."

"I bet it was." She kept her replies simple.

Lily pulled back and looked at Josie. "My dad misses my mom, you know. He's very lonely."

"I'm sure he is." Josie gave her a gentle smile and wiped a smudge of dust off her nose, refusing to get pulled into a discussion about Silas.

Lily sighed, as if sensing Josie's reluctance, then Alyssa called her and she was off again.

But as Josie walked back to where her grandmother waited, voicing her impatience, her thoughts drifted back to Silas. Imagining him with Lily. Imagining him alone.

Chapter Eight

"I had a lot of fun at Ms. Josie's place," Lily announced as she carried her overnight bag into the house. "Can I go again?"

Silas followed her, dropping his own bag onto the kitchen floor. "Maybe. Sometime."

"We had so much fun," she said as she set her bag on the kitchen table. She carefully pulled out her folded clothes while she chattered. "Ms. Josie said to treat these clothes with respect 'cause they were a special gift. And I got them from you for my birthday." She shot him a gleaming smile. "And Ms. Josie helped me with my homework. She's really smart and really pretty and I really like her…" Her endless chatter faded away.

Thankfully. He didn't want to be treated to yet another listing of Ms. Josie's more obvious attributes. He was fully aware that she was smart and pretty. Too aware in fact.

He pulled out a frozen pizza and peeled the wrapping off.

"I have to find my…my…" Lily's sentence trailed off again as she dug through her bag.

"What do you have to you find?" he prompted, thankful they were now on another topic.

But Lily shook her head, sat back, took a breath and

charged onward. "Ms. Josie's Gramma is grumpy, and when I told her that I liked my new clothes she said that God looks at the heart and not at the clothes, then I told her God probably liked my clothes. Then we sang some really neat songs. I even remembered one. Mommy used to— I mean, I used to sing it. It's the song about Jesus loving all the children of the world and it made me feel happy that Jesus loves me. The minister told all the kids a story about memories and how we have good memories and bad memories and that it's important to hold on—"

"What do you mean, 'the minister'?" Silas asked, letting the oven door slam shut as her chatter registered.

"Reverend Garrison." Lily frowned at him. "You know. The minister who works at the church."

"You went to church on Sunday?" He didn't mean for his voice to come out so hard. What was Josie thinking to take his daughter to church without telling him?

"We went to the Old Town Hall, too," she continued, though the excitement had been leached out of her voice. She let a careful smile slip over her mouth, as if testing his tolerance and when he didn't say anything, carried on. "You and mommy were married in the Old Town Hall, and at Ms. Josie's house me and Alyssa played Bride and Groom. I pretended I was the Bride, and Alyssa pretended she was you. But she's smaller and she doesn't have cowboy boots like you do, of course."

Silas pressed back his comments, struggling with his reaction to her blithe recital.

"But the Old Town Hall isn't ready. Josie said they don't have enough people to help. Why don't you help, Daddy? Then maybe it can be ready on time."

Silas took two plates out of the cupboard and dropped them on the table. "I don't have time."

"But if they don't get enough people, it won't be ready for Founders' Day." Lily injected an extra note of entreaty into her voice, which usually melted away even his most firm resolve.

He didn't want to rebuild the Old Town Hall. In fact, he had seen it as some type of divine retribution that it was leveled during the storm. It seemed appropriate that the place he and Kelly had begun the wonderful life they didn't have anymore had been reduced to rubble.

"Why don't you wash up and bring your clothes to your room? Supper will be ready soon."

She frowned at him, but thankfully did as she was told.

A couple hours later he had brought Lily to bed and, at her insistence, had sung the song again. Then she had insisted on praying, telling him that maybe Mommy was listening.

Sentimental claptrap. But he suffered through it, did what she asked because he knew she wouldn't quit until he did, then bid her good night.

As he closed the door, however, he felt a flash of irritation with the lovely Josie Cane for putting him in this situation. For the first few months after Kelly's death, Lily wanted him to pray with her. He couldn't. She had left him alone after that.

Now it looked like they were back at it again. He'd have to talk to Miss Cane about this. But first he had work to do. A farm to maintain.

He worked on the brochure for his sale for an hour, then, when he was fairly sure Lily was asleep, he went downstairs and got on the phone.

Josie answered on the third ring. She sounded breathless.

"Did I catch you at a bad time?" he asked, planting one hand on his hip, the other clenching the handset of the phone. *Relax. Don't get overemotional.*

"No. I was just putting my grandmother in bed."

Of course. The unselfish Josie Cane busy with her cantankerous grandmother. Through dinner he'd got to hear a few more stories from Lily about Betty Carter and he found himself alternately feeling sorry for Josie and feeling admiration for her patience.

"What can I do for you, Silas?"

He hesitated, suddenly unsure of how to proceed, then decided that his priority was Lily. Not Josie's feelings. "I understand you took Lily to the Old Town Hall."

"You understand correctly."

"We've had this discussion before. About bringing up the past."

This netted him silence on Josie's part. Maybe it was getting through to her.

"I'm sorry, Silas," she said finally. "I can't agree."

He frowned. "What do you mean?"

"In your mind your wife's death is in the past. Done. Over," Josie said. "But not in Lily's. She still has memories and sorrows, and I think it's dangerous to put a lid on those and expect her to be in the same emotional place you are."

"I'm only trying to protect my daughter from pain that she can't understand."

"Or are you trying to protect yourself?"

This got him peeved. "And where did you get your psychology degree?"

"The University of Life, Mr. Marstow," Josie snapped.

In spite of his irritation with her, he had to smile. *Touché*, he thought.

"Regardless of what you think, Lily is my daughter." He shoved his hand through his hair as he tried to regain his footing in this discussion.

"And Lily was in my home, and I have my own ideas. I think Lily needs to know about her past and you need to face it."

Silas bit back an angry reply, feeling as if Josie was pushing him into a corner. But then he fought back.

"What about taking her to church? Is that why you offered to take her in? So you could indoctrinate her?"

"Hardly indoctrination. Merely reintroducing her to something she'd already been exposed to. She told me she used to attend church."

"Emphasis on *used to*." He stopped there. He didn't need to explain himself to her.

"Why did you stop going?"

Silas pulled his hand over his face, realizing he had made a tactical error. He shouldn't have started this conversation. He should have said what he needed to say and then said goodbye.

But now he was stuck talking to her. He should have known that conversation with women was tricky and unknown territory, a place where a mere male could easily get lost.

"Doesn't matter." He hoped his terse reply would shut this down.

"But I think it does," Josie said, her voice lowering as if she was all concerned. "Because Lily used to go and she misses going."

"Why do you care? Why does this matter so much to you?" He dropped into a chair, resting his elbows on the kitchen table.

More silence and once again he regretted his outburst. He was doing okay, being all stoic and concise, but she just wouldn't quit.

"It matters because…because I see in Lily some of the yearning that I faced at one time in my life. A yearning for family and for memories and for the solidity of a faith heritage!" She paused and Silas sincerely hoped this was the end of the discussion. Things were getting shakier and shakier. "My own parents died when I was young. My grandmother wouldn't talk about my parents either and, well, I think I needed to know those stories, to know my parents and to know how their faith sustained them through hard times. I think I needed to know what God gave them so I could come back…" Her voice faded away and Silas knew she was referring to her own shady past.

Silas endured an all-too-familiar moment of pain and he fought it down. "God doesn't give," he snapped. "God takes. God takes your time, your money and your prayers. And then He takes your wife."

He stopped himself there, frustrated that he'd shown her even a glimpse of what he'd struggled with ever since his wife died.

In the silence that followed, Silas felt like hanging up. This conversation was a waste of time.

But he didn't. He waited to see what Josie would say to his heretical statement. She was probably waiting for the lightning to strike.

"God didn't take Kelly away, Silas. Cancer took Kelly away."

Her quiet but forceful words slipped into the crack he had shown her. Settled onto the painful memories he had skirted around so many times.

He didn't know what to say. No one had ever challenged him like she had or made him talk like she had.

He didn't like it.

Her gentle sigh sifted through the phone line. Had she regretted her sudden outburst?

"I also thought you should know that Lily brought a photo album here. It had a picture of Kelly on the front."

Silas swallowed. Then again. He was pretty sure he knew which album it was. Kelly's sister had made it for Lily shortly after Kelly died. Silas couldn't bear to see it and had hid it in his room.

At least he thought he had hid it in his room.

"I'm sorry if I stepped out of line," Josie said, sounding uncharacteristically contrite. "I'm just concerned about Lily and I'm concerned about—" She stopped there.

Silas waited for her to finish the sentence.

"Sorry, Silas, but I think in the matter of Kelly, you're

wrong. As for God, I think it's wrong to keep Lily away from Him, as well. Especially when God wants too much to be with us in our times of sorrow."

Silas's grip on the handset tightened as his anger shifted, lessened.

"Do you really believe God cared, Josie? Do you really think we matter to Him?"

"With all my heart."

He couldn't answer her; then, into the silence humming over the airwaves, she whispered, "Goodbye."

Silas stared at the handset as—in spite of his tough words—her own took root.

He put the phone down, then on a whim, walked upstairs. He stopped by Lily's bedroom door. He turned the knob and carefully pushed open the door.

In the triangle of light he created, he saw Lily curled up on her side, her head tipped back, mouth open. She had kicked the blankets off and her one foot hung over the edge of the bed.

She was holding something square. Curious, he walked closer, avoiding the squeaky floorboard just inside the door.

He crouched down and gently lifted her arm. He recognized the album. It was the one Josie said Lily had taken to her place.

Was his daughter really pining for her mother? Had he been wrong in trying to keep the memories at bay?

As he watched his daughter, a memory slipped into his mind. Kelly standing beside him in this very room, watching with him as they looked down on Lily. Kelly had just been given the final, chilling prognosis.

His lovely wife was dying.

They had stood, watching their innocent daughter, her life so uncomplicated, both knowing the darkness that would fall on her.

Then, Kelly had put her arms around him and extracted a

promise that he wouldn't stay single forever. That he would find someone to help take care of Lily. That, God willing, he would give Lily a complete family again.

He'd ignored her, pushed her comment away into the pit of denial he'd put everything to do with her disease.

And now, in spite of his determination to carry on, to push forward, to forget, the memory had slipped out.

It was Josie's fault. Pain threaded through his soul and breached his defenses. She was the one who had opened the lid of the box he had tried to keep shut.

Do You really care, God, he silently cried out, staring down at his daughter, remembering her sorrow.

He hadn't shed a tear since he found out Kelly had been diagnosed. He'd soldiered on. Strong. Stoic.

But as he stood beside Lily's bed, memories flooded his soul. Memories of Kelly praying for him and Lily. Praying for herself. Kelly's trust in God had been absolute and it had never wavered.

Silas closed his eyes against the pain, but he couldn't hold it back.

He pressed his hands to his face as a sob slipped through his fingers. Then another.

Why did You do this, Lord? Why did You take her away? What had she ever done to You? She was goodness and kindness and love.

Silas swayed, then slipped to the floor, leaning back against the bed.

And in the silence, his daughter sleeping innocently above him, he silently released his grief and his tears.

It hurt, it was ugly. He fought to control it and lost.

He cried for the loss of his dreams, he cried for what his daughter had lost. He cried for each grimace of pain he had seen on his lovely wife's face, he cried for each smile she gave him through her suffering.

And he cried for what he had lost.

God didn't take your wife away. Cancer did.

Josie's words echoed through his sorrow and in spite of the tears coursing down his cheeks, he felt a sense of rightness about her words.

It had been easier to blame God than to accept the stark reality that Kelly was simply gone.

Silas palmed the moisture off his cheeks, glancing backward. Lily slept on, her mouth still open, her fingers twitching in her sleep.

So innocent, and so vulnerable.

I just wanted to keep the pain away from her, he thought as he got to his knees beside her bed. I didn't want her to feel my sorrow. My hurt.

Forgive me, Lord, he prayed.

It was all he could say for now. Silas wasn't naive enough to think a few tears would erase the anger he still felt when he thought of Kelly's struggles. But this was a small step.

As he knelt by his daughter's bed, much like he and Kelly had done each night that she was able, a gentle prayer soothed him, granted him the forgiveness and the peace he'd yearned for.

Lily shifted in her bed. As she threw her arm over her head, the book she'd been protecting slipped onto the floor and fell open.

Silas glanced down at it, bracing himself to see pictures of his dear wife. Bracing himself for the pain he might feel again.

Instead Josie Cane stared back at him, her face full of laughter and fun. Silas bent over and turned another page and saw another picture of Josie.

A curious tension seized him. Had Lily replaced all of her mother's pictures with pictures of Josie? He thought of the present Lily had given him for his birthday. What was she trying to do?

He flipped to the front of the album and felt a mixture of relief and familiar sorrow.

Kelly's pictures still filled the front of the album. Josie's the back empty pages.

What was going on?

Chapter Nine

"**Y**our parents are coming, let's clean up." Josie clapped her hands to get the childrens' attention, then walked around the room, supervising. In a matter of minutes books were put away, the play centers were tidied up and order was restored.

Just how she liked it, Josie thought. She caught sight of one of her students.

"Tommy, can you come here a minute?" He trudged over and she tucked his shirt in, then retied his shoelace. "Don't want you falling down," she said, touching the tip of his nose just as the door opened. The first parents had arrived.

She helped sort out backpacks and jackets, picked up papers that fell out and caught up with the mothers who had come.

A few minutes later it was only Alyssa and Lily, who sat on a table, swinging her legs. "My daddy needs a new watch," Lily said, her narrow shoulders lifting in a dramatic sigh. Then she brightened. "Maybe I can come to your place again?"

Or not, Josie thought, remembering too well the conversation she and Silas had had last night.

"Your daddy won't forget." Josie took the barrette out of Lily's hair, finger-combed the strands back into some semblance of order, then reclipped it.

Lily's eyes flew to the door and she jumped off the table. "Daddy. You came."

Silas stood in the doorway, his presence filling the space, dominating the room. He wore a cowboy hat today and combined with his plaid shirt, faded blue jeans and scuffed cowboy boots, he looked as if he had stepped right out of a Western movie.

His gaze caught Josie's, held it for a beat, then he looked down at Lily who was now clinging to his free hand.

Josie smoothed her hands over her cotton skirt, cleared her throat, stilled the goofy, little lift of her heart and walked toward Silas.

"Lily, go wait for me in the truck," Silas said.

"Can Alyssa come with me?" Lily asked, swinging his hand back and forth.

Silas nodded, his eyes back on Josie. He released his daughter's hand and pulled his hat off his head. The gesture seemed courtly and from another generation and it stole into Josie's heart.

Alyssa squealed and together the friends ran out the door, leaving an expectant silence in their wake.

Josie waited until she saw them at Silas's truck, parked in front of the church, then she turned to Silas.

He shifted his weight, leaning his shoulder against the door frame.

She was about to apologize for interfering but he spoke first. "I've been thinking," he said. "About Lily missing Kelly. And maybe you're right." He blew out his breath, as if unsure of how to carry on, his eyes on hers.

Josie fought the urge to talk. To fill the silence. He needed the space to speak the words she saw hovering in his eyes.

"Maybe she does miss her," he said finally. "What do I do? She's gone. How do I fix that? I can't bring Kelly back. I can't take away the pain."

Josie felt a burst of pity for his heartfelt plea and suspected part of his confusion was about his own sorrow and his own pain.

"You don't need to take it away, Silas," she said quietly. "You just need to know it's there. To know that it's a part of you and it's a part of Lily. And then to let God heal that pain."

Silas's gaze drifted sideways, as if seeking some other solution. "God again," he said quietly.

"God again."

But she was relieved to see a faint smile tease one corner of his mouth. "You don't quit with that, do you?"

"Mostly because God doesn't quit. I've found that out in my own life."

Silas nodded, pushed himself away from the door frame and to her surprise took a step nearer.

"You really believe that God can make a difference? That God can help?"

"I do," she said quietly, his nearness creating a curious fluttering in her abdomen. Well, not so curious. She had felt this before, but not since high school.

He emitted a short laugh, then nodded. "And do you think Lily will be helped by that?"

"I know she will. Children have an amazing ability to rebound and to trust. But in order for that to happen, we have to be completely honest with them. Always."

"There's another thing that concerns me even more." Silas cleared his throat and looked away from Josie, his hands working their way around the brim of his hat. "I have a few concerns about your relationship with Lily. I think she's getting too attached."

"I am one of her teachers," Josie reminded him. "At this age, it's not unusual for girls to be attached to their teachers."

"But I'm thinking it's unhealthy. Especially because of…Kelly."

"Attachments are a healthy part of life, Silas," Josie said, trying to make her point in a rational and quiet way.

"I know you're worried about her memories of Kelly, but can I hazard a guess that she's further along the grieving process than you are?"

Silas slapped his hat against the side of his leg again, his eyes delving into hers.

"If you're going to be leaving I'm not sure she should get so attached."

Josie crossed her arms over her chest, struggling to hold her words back. "Are you saying you want to take her out of the program?"

Silas shook his head. "No. Not after I said she could stay. It's just, I'm worried. Getting too close to you will only cause her hurt. Or pain. That's the reality."

"That's not reality. I think that's escape. And I think *that's* unhealthy both for Lily and for you."

Silas clenched his jaw and for a moment Josie knew she had crossed a line.

But for some reason, she didn't care. She felt so badly for Lily and Silas. He was cutting himself off from people—from God—and that bothered her more than she wanted to examine right now.

"I'm not escaping." He scratched his forehead with a finger as he slowly shook his head. "Last night..." He paused, then ended the sentence on a sigh.

What was he going to say?

Then his gaze delved into hers and in his eyes she saw his deep, broken places.

Her hand lifted from her side to reach out to him. But she caught herself. They didn't have that kind of relationship and to bridge the gap between them in this way would be to move into territory she wasn't sure she should enter.

But she couldn't leave the conversation like this. She felt compelled to say more. "Maybe not, but I know you keep to yourself. I don't think that's good."

"Kelly used to say life is lived in community, but..."

This small glimpse into his past gave her hope. And she wanted to build on the scrap he had given her.

"She was right. Community is one of the ways God shows us His love." She gestured to the Old Town Hall. "Your daughter was so happy to find out the hall is getting fixed up and so worried that it wouldn't happen in time for Founders' Day. She has a built-in sense of community and I think she wants to be involved. Maybe you need to be involved, too. Maybe it's how you can find a way to heal."

"Maybe. But my bigger concern right now is Lily."

"How so?" Josie sensed he was moving to another place.

"I don't want Lily to be hurt."

"In what way?"

"You said Lily was carrying around an album that held pictures of Kelly."

"She brought it to my house when she stayed overnight."

Silas scratched his cheek with one fingernail. "I found her sleeping with the album last night." His voice was heavy with unspoken feelings.

Pity gripped Josie's heart with a heavy hand. "I'm so sorry, Silas—"

He held his hand up, his expression puzzled. "The album wasn't holding only pictures of my wife. Half of it had pictures of you."

Josie stared at him while his words registered in her brain, quite sure her mouth was slipping open in surprise. "What are you talking about? What pictures of me?" She had seen the album. Knew exactly what it held.

"They were just random photos. Some were old. Looked like they were from high school."

Pictures of her? Did he think she put them in there?

A warm flush crept up her neck at the thought. She was sure her cheeks were a cherry-red. "I'm sorry. I have no idea how they got there."

Silas sighed. "This makes things a bit awkward, you

know. I also got a picture of you from Lily for my birthday. I didn't think anything of it at the time, but now I'm wondering what is going on."

By now the flush had reached her hairline. Great. She probably looked like a candy cane. Red face. White hair.

What if he thought she was behind this? "I'm sorry, I had nothing to do with this."

"I'm pretty sure you didn't." Then he cleared his throat, pushed his hat back on his head and shot a glance over his shoulder at the girls. They were watching them with avid interest.

Josie had a pretty good idea what had happened.

"If you don't mind my being a bit forward—" Josie said, knowing she needed to articulate her suspicions.

"A bit?" He lifted one eyebrow in a gesture of incredulity.

"Okay, a lot." She lifted her hands as if showing him she wasn't holding back this time, either. "I think I know exactly what is going on."

His frown told her that he still hadn't clued in.

Men.

Josie sighed. She was hoping she wouldn't have to spell it out.

"You are concerned about Lily getting attached to me. Well, I think it's worse than that. I think the girls are playing matchmaker," she said with a light laugh, just in case he thought she was an active participant.

Silas tipped his head to one side as if considering this new wrinkle.

"I'm going to have a talk with Alyssa once you're gone," she continued, hating the breathlessness of her voice. "And I suggest you talk to Lily. Of course she may not be in on this, but, well…it wouldn't hurt to mention it to her, too. In case she is. In on it, that is."

Stop, stop before he either thinks you really are involved or he thinks you're a complete idiot.

"I'll do that," he said carefully. "But how, I'm not sure."

"Just keep it straightforward. That's the best strategy." She stepped back, hoping the physical distance would give her some mental space. "Thanks for stopping by, Mr. Marstow."

A light frown creased his forehead, as if puzzled at her sudden withdrawal. "You're welcome, *Josie.*" His voice laid a gentle emphasis on the last word and he added a quizzical smile to his reply.

Then he turned and left.

Josie wrapped her arms around herself as she watched him jog down the steps of the church, two at a time. She felt herself relax, as if she'd been holding on to something heavy she could finally put down.

Had she said the right thing? Done the right thing?

What were those silly girls thinking? She suddenly felt incredibly foolish. Here she thought Lily was carting an album around because she missed her mother.

What child wouldn't? She knew that she did after her parents died. How long did it take before you were ready to move on? Days? Weeks?

Josie rubbed her forehead. Had she stuck her nose in business that she had no right to be involved in?

Yet, at the same time, she knew she had done the right thing in encouraging Silas to go to the past. To let Lily learn the stories of her mother. To let them enrich her life.

Dear Lord, she prayed, *give me wisdom in this situation. Show me what I should do.*

And don't let him think I'm in any way involved in what the girls are doing.

But as Silas drove away, she watched until he made that last turn and she couldn't see his truck anymore.

Josie didn't say anything to Alyssa on their way home, nor during dinner.

But when Alyssa was done saying her prayers, Josie stayed perched on the edge of her niece's bed. She stroked

Alyssa's hair back, thinking, once again, how much like Lily's it was. No wonder people often mistook them for twins.

An image, unbidden, slipped into her mind. Alyssa and Lily wearing matching outfits, their hair done the same. How cute would that be?

Josie reined her thoughts back, making herself return to the plans she had been working on—before. Since the tornado her life had been turned as upside down as her house.

All her time was taken up with keeping her life stable, dealing with the insurance company on her house, and dealing with her grandmother who, even now, was calling out for her.

"Be right with you, Gramma," Josie called out, pressing down her impatience. She turned back to Alyssa and gave her niece a careful smile.

"Alyssa, honey, you and Lily are good friends, aren't you?"

Alyssa nodded, her hands folded over the sheet covering her chest. "We're the bestest of friends, almost like sisters. And I know *bestest* isn't a word, but it's a good word."

Josie tucked a stray lock of Alyssa's hair back behind her ear. "I think it's a good word for what you and Lily share. But you're just friends, you know?"

Alyssa nodded, no trace of guile in her expression.

Josie smiled to take away the disappointment of her next statement. "And that's probably all you'll ever be."

Confusion flickered in Alyssa's eyes and Josie realized she needed to come at this head-on.

"Lily brought a photo album here," she stated. "The one with pictures of her mother."

Alyssa nodded, but guilt colored her cheeks. Josie waited for Alyssa to say something, then realized she had to take her own advice. She went for straightforward.

"Who put the pictures of me in that album?"

Alyssa's eyes grew wide and her mouth formed a perfect O. "What… How…?"

"Mr. Marstow found the album in Lily's bed. And he opened it up." Josie folded her hands on her lap, praying for the right way to approach this without making Alyssa feel as if she had done something bad. She understood Alyssa's misguided motives. How often had she heard Alyssa's innocent comparisons of their family to those of most of her friends? Friends who had father and mother and often a sibling or two?

Alyssa often commented on the fact that she and Josie were alone and how nice it would be to have a man to help with the hard stuff. But Josie had to explain that this was not the way to go about creating Alyssa's little dream.

"I was wondering why there were pictures of me in that album?" she asked.

Alyssa's gaze flicked away and her fingers twisted around each other. "Lily likes you" was her quiet response.

Josie said nothing, knowing her silence would be more effective at drawing the information out.

"…and…well…we thought…I thought…" Alyssa's hesitating followed by a trembling sigh almost made Josie feel sorry for her. Until she thought of Silas paging through the album looking at who knows what kinds of pictures of her.

"…we thought…me and Lily made a deal. She called it a pact. We wanted to get you and Mr. Marstow together." Alyssa pushed herself up. "I wanted a dad and Lily wanted a mom and she tells me how lonely he is and how she has to eat lousy sandwiches all the time and that she doesn't want to see him sad anymore. She said he sits on the porch at night, staring out at the stars and he looks so by himself. Sometimes he sits there all night."

The picture Alyssa drew created a subtle undertow of pity for the little girl who would sit and watch her father by himself at night. And for the father. For a moment she wished she could ease that loneliness. With a start she drew herself back to the present. She had no right to be thinking about Silas that way.

"But you can't make that decision for big people," Josie said quietly. "You can't just pick a dad and Lily can't just pick a mom."

"But Lily said that Mr. Marstow thinks you're pretty."

The innocent comment brought back her blush in full bloom. Thankfully Josie was sitting with her back to the light coming from the hallway into the room.

"That's nice, but that doesn't mean we should get... together."

"I know that," Alyssa said with a faint note of scorn in her voice. "But it helps, right? And Mr. Marstow is very good-looking, isn't he?"

"Well, yes. He is." Her blush deepened as she thought of the shared moment in the doorway of the church that afternoon.

"Then it's perfect." Alyssa clasped her hands together in front of her in her exuberance.

"Honey, it doesn't matter how good-looking he is or whether he thinks I'm pretty or not." Josie felt as if she was walking blind, unsure of what Alyssa would throw out and uncertain of exactly how to respond. She didn't want her niece building castles in the air on some offhand comment she made nor was she ready to break the news to her niece about her plans to leave. "It matters what is in our hearts. God also looks at our hearts and that's what is more important."

"But you have a good heart and you love Jesus," Alyssa pressed.

"Yes, and that is more important to me than anything." Josie latched on to the argument, thankful she had something solid to cling to. "And I don't know if Mr. Marstow loves Jesus like I do."

"But what if he wants to go to church? I could tell Lily to

ask him to go to church and maybe he could learn to love Jesus and then you and him could—"

Josie put her finger on Alyssa's lips. It was a parental last-ditch effort to extricate herself from this tricky discussion.

"We're not talking about this anymore, okay?" Josie leveled her a steady look, hoping the sternness in her voice underlined the seriousness of the situation. "You and Lily are good friends, but that's it. You're not doing any more match-making. Do you understand?"

Alyssa opened her mouth, but Josie pressed lightly on her lips and Alyssa ducked her head. "Yes. I understand."

"Good. Now let's get you tucked in again and then you can go to sleep."

"Can you sing with me?" Alyssa asked, a plaintive note threaded through her voice.

Josie relented. "Of course I can."

They sang "Jesus Tender Shepherd," then a song that Josie's mother had taught her and Alyssa's mother. When they were done, Alyssa was smiling.

"Good night, sweetheart," Josie said, bending over to kiss her.

"Good night, Auntie Josie," Alyssa said, snuggling deeper into her blankets.

Josie got up and just as she got to the door Alyssa called her name.

Josie turned. "What is it, my dear?"

"Do you think Mr. Marstow sings to Lily at night?"

Josie shook her head to show Alyssa the subject was finished, then closed the door. *Persistent little stinker.*

But as she leaned back against the door, her niece's innocent question thrummed through her mind. She tried to imagine Silas singing to Lily. The picture wouldn't gel.

But she easily imagined him sitting on the deck. Staring out into the night. All alone.

Chapter Ten

"I'm bringing lunch to the men working at the Old Town Hall. Will you be okay?" Josie stood in the doorway of the living room, holding a platter of wrapped sandwiches.

Betty Carter glanced up from her jigsaw puzzle. "I guess I will. Allison said she was coming by in half an hour, so I hope I don't get too bored." Her grandmother's eyes flicked over the tray. "Those working men get hungry. Are you sure you got enough food there?"

Josie chose to sidestep the barb her grandmother threw at her. "I'll be back in an hour or so." Then, without waiting to hear another negative response, she left the house.

Thankfully the sun had some extra warmth today to offset the chill she always got from her grandmother. Josie didn't know if she was growing hypersensitive to her grandmother's goading or if her grandmother was simply growing more and more cantankerous because of living in such close quarters. Either way it required more and more grace to put up with Betty Carter.

Josie walked as quickly as she could with the heavy tray, wondering if, as her grandmother had intimated, she had enough sandwiches.

As she got near the building a vehicle pulled up and Greg

Garrison got out. But he didn't see her and strode into the building, a man with a clipboard and a mission. Josie assumed he was there to find out what materials they might need from his lumber supply yard.

She went to the back of the building, where she usually entered. Lexi was already there setting up a makeshift table in what Josie assumed was to be the new kitchen of the hall.

"Hey, Josie, thanks for coming early," Lexi said looking up from the cloth she was laying down on the piece of plywood that served as a table. "I can't stay too long. I've got a dog coming to the clinic in twenty minutes."

"How many men are here today?" Josie asked as she set the tray down.

Lexi gave her a sly look as she set out the cups. "One more than yesterday."

"That's good," Josie replied, unsure why Lexi was grinning the way she was. "We've been running short of volunteers."

"Here's cream and sugar. Nicki brought some drinks and a pan of squares. She'll be bringing them in a minute."

"Is Colt helping today?" Josie asked, unwrapping the sandwiches.

"He had to check out on a vandalism report." Lexi's smile grew soft.

"Now that you two are back together again, Reverend Garrison doesn't have you and Colt working the same volunteer shifts here?"

"It is funny. Isn't it?" Lexi glanced over the table, then up at Josie. "And it is funny how Silas suddenly is."

"What are you talking about?"

Lexi palmed her question aside. "Nothing. Nothing at all. I gotta go."

As she left, Josie walked out of the kitchen into the main hall area.

The last time she and the girls had been here it was quiet.

Now the sound of a pneumatic hammer slammed through the piercing whine of a power saw.

In the center of the room, Greg Garrison and his cousin Michael were consulting Greg's clipboard. A hard hat covered Michael's usually unruly hair but Greg was bareheaded.

But Josie's gaze only skimmed over the other men, Klaas Steenbergen, a neighbor of hers and Hal Triskell, an old schoolmate of hers. Her eyes sought and easily found Silas. He was kneeling on the floor, pushing a piece of hardwood snug against another while Hal nailed the wood with a nail gun.

"We'll put this last piece in and then quit for lunch," Hal said, walking over with another board. He set it down, rolled his neck and stretched his tattooed arms out in front of him.

As if sensing her presence, Silas glanced up from the board he was nailing. His eyes caught hers and held.

Awareness hovered between them, as ethereal as the sawdust motes dancing in the air. Her throat thickened and her heartbeat stepped up its flighty rhythm.

"Marstow, quit staring at Josie." Hal aimed a sly wink Josie's way. "She comes every day, you know."

Michael and Greg Garrison both stopped their conversation, looking at the two of them.

She knew she was blushing. She felt the heat sliding up her neck. Again.

Josie spun around and forced herself not to run to the kitchen. What was with this man? She hadn't blushed in years. Not even when she'd done things she should have blushed about.

Now, in the space of a couple of days, she'd been flushing like a prissy Victorian miss.

Which she definitely wasn't, she thought as she put out paper plates for the men to use for their lunch.

Now the hammer was quiet, the saw had shut down and from the hall she heard the quiet voice of the minister discuss what they would do after lunch.

The other door to the kitchen opened and Nicki stepped in carrying a platter of squares balanced on one hand and a large jug of juice in another.

"Great. Some help," Josie said with forced brightness. She didn't want to face Silas on her own. Not after what she had just experienced.

Nicki dropped the tray and the jug on the table and took a couple steps back. "Sorry, friend. I've got to get back to the kids. But there are not that many guys. You should be okay."

"Yeah. Just great," Josie said with a wan smile.

Nicki frowned, but Josie flapped her hands at her in a shooing motion. "Don't leave the kids alone. You get going."

The door barely closed on Nicki when the men entered the kitchen.

"Another great spread put on by the lovely women of High Plains." Hal rubbed his hands together, the lion tattooed on the back of his hand flexing with the movement. "And none lovelier than our own Josie Cane."

"This looks really good, Josie," Reverend Michael Garrison said as he slipped the hard hat off his head. "Why don't we have a word of thanks before we eat?"

Hal stopped himself, and pulled his own hard hat off, revealing a shaved head, shiny with sweat.

Josie wasn't going to look at Silas, but out of the corner of her eye she saw him pull his hand back and take his hard hat off, as well.

"Thank You, Lord, for this food, for the hands that prepared it," the minister prayed. "Thank You for the help we have in rebuilding this hall. Help us each day to realize the many blessings You have given us, and to look to You for all our needs. Thank You for the community You have placed us in. May we build each other up for You. Amen."

A moment of silence followed, and then Hal dropped his hard hat on the floor. "Let's eat. I'm starving."

"Please, help yourself," Josie said as she unwrapped the

sandwiches, meticulously folding the plastic wrap as the men reached for the food.

Klaas filled up his plate then slipped into the main room to eat.

"These sandwiches look great, Josie," Reverend Michael was saying as the door fell shut behind Klaas.

Josie glanced up and caught Reverend Michael's smile. She tried not to read anything into his grin. He was just being friendly, she reminded herself.

"How long will you be helping today?" she asked him as she poured coffee and juice into the cups.

"I'm just scamming some lunch and then I'm gone."

"So you just stayed long enough to eat?" she asked with a light laugh.

"Pretty much." He loaded up his plate. "See ya, guys. I'm off to my other job." He edged backward out the door, his hands full, but just before he left, he glanced at Silas, then winked at Josie.

She looked away, directly into the eyes of Silas Marstow. Great. Had he caught Michael's silent innuendo?

"I didn't know lunch was provided," Silas said as he helped himself to a couple of sandwiches.

"Did you pack a lunch?"

He shook his head. "I was going to head over to one of the fast-food places in town."

"This is faster," Hal said. "And Josie is much easier on the eyes than anyone you'll find at those places."

"Hal, sorry to bother you at lunchtime, but I need to double-check the order for the rest of the hardwood flooring before I leave." Greg Garrison stood in the doorway of the kitchen, holding his clipboard.

Hal grabbed his full plate and sauntered out of the kitchen with Greg, leaving Silas and Josie behind.

"You come here every day?" Silas asked, dropping into one of the empty chairs Josie had set out.

"I try to." She poured some coffee for herself, feeling the need to do something with her hands. Why did she feel so ill at ease all of a sudden around this man?

"Yet another one of your volunteer duties?" Silas asked.

The faint teasing note in his voice eased away the tension tightening her shoulders. "Of course. I am indispensable in this town," she said with a light laugh.

"Seems that way." Silas took a drink of coffee.

"I don't come every day." Josie sat down in a chair on the other side of the table. "And now you're volunteering, as well?"

"Lily started in on me about helping with the Old Town Hall." Silas turned his hand over, palm up in a what-can-I-do gesture. "She seems to have more time to nag than I have time to tell her I don't have time to help. So here I am."

"I'm glad you decided to help." Josie took a sip of coffee, holding the cup with two hands.

"I don't know if this place will get done on time. I thought there'd be way more people helping."

"There were. At first, but I think we're running into volunteer fatigue." Josie looked up just as he glanced over at her. She looked away. "I know Reverend Garrison is in contact with a church group from Manhattan that is talking about coming up to help out. We'll see. Trouble is there are people who aren't even living in their own homes yet, so I'm thinking that might be a priority."

"People like you and Alyssa?"

Silas's quiet question slipped in behind her fragile defenses. "I guess."

"What's happening with your house?"

Josie looked into the steaming coffee, as if hoping she could find a solution there. "Nothing. That's the trouble. I can't get any more work done on the house until the work that has been done is inspected and approved. This morning I sent away yet another set of forms for the insurance company. Hopefully this time I did it right."

"Do you need a hand with the paperwork? I don't know lots about insurance companies but I've had to make a couple of claims on the ranch."

"That's fine," Josie said. "I can manage."

She looked up to see Silas shaking his head, his eyes on her. "You are allowed to let other people help you, you know," he said. "Someone told me that once."

"That someone is a nosey parker who should mind her own business."

"I thought it was good advice. That's why I used it and am now passing it on."

"I'll see what happens in the next few days." Josie finished her coffee and got up. Only there wasn't anything to do until the men went back to work. So she took a sandwich herself and sat down again.

"You seem nervous," Silas said. "Something wrong?"

Josie took a bite of her sandwich and shrugged. Something was wrong and she wasn't exactly sure when she had become so aware of Silas and so uncomfortable in his presence.

"Your grandmother okay?"

She nodded.

"Lily said that she liked to complain a lot."

"My grandmother has had her difficulties," Josie said, defending Betty. "I wasn't exactly easy on her."

"And now you're taking care of your sister's girl."

"Since she was two." Josie took a chance and shot him a quick glance and a smile. "And I do it gladly."

"I can see that. Alyssa seems like a nice girl. I know with Lily, it's Alyssa this and Alyssa that. Kinda cute. I'm glad she has a good friend."

"What are you two lovebirds chitchatting about?" Hal burst into the kitchen and made for the sandwich platter. "Something you want to share with old Hal?" he said, lifting his eyebrows at Josie.

"Just sandwiches and coffee, Hal," Josie returned, fixing him with a steady look.

She had never cared for Hal and she was fairly sure the feeling was mutual. Hal had been at any number of parties she had attended as a young girl and every now and then he liked to act as if she hadn't changed. As if she was the same wild girl she had been back in the day.

Hal dropped into a chair and leaned it back on two legs. "I hear you're starting a dude ranch on your place?" he asked Silas.

As Silas replied, the talk shifted to work and making a living. Josie found out Silas was in the process of building some cabins on his place but that he was short of lumber, which had all been diverted to work on the town. The ordinary talk served to make her feel more relaxed around Silas.

A few minutes later Klaas came back with his cup and plate. Hal lurched to his feet and patted his stomach. "Great lunch, Josie," he said. "And good company."

He waggled his eyebrows at her, then laughed and left.

Silas got up and put his plate on the table. "I'll probably be picking up Lily right from school today," he said. "I know she doesn't want to miss her after-school program, but I can't stay away from the farm too long."

"Of course. I understand." Josie glanced up at him, pleased that she could hold his gaze without even a hint of self-consciousness.

Then he gave her a cautious smile. "I'm really glad I came to work here," he said, buckling up his carpenter belt. "I think…I think Kelly would approve."

His easy mention of his wife gave her a glimmer of hope.

"I think she would, too," Josie said quietly, holding his gaze.

He didn't look away and she couldn't.

Then, to her utter surprise, he raised his gloved hand and laid it gently on her shoulder. "Thanks, Josie." He tightened his grip, his eyes locked on hers.

The air between them seeped away, replaced by unspoken words and questions.

Then he left, leaving her feeling slightly shaken by something as casual as a light touch.

"Soup today?" Silas took a plastic bowl and handed it to Josie.

"It's cold out. You men need to keep up your strength." Josie poured a ladle full of the steaming soup into the bowl and added a gentle smile.

He held her gaze a beat longer than necessary and Josie willed herself not to blush or to remember the little moment yesterday. When he'd touched her.

Josie knew at what cost Silas had done that. She knew what he had been fighting.

At this stage of life these small movements were more important than they were when she was a foolish teenager flirting with any male that would pay attention to her.

She wasn't that girl anymore.

And Silas wasn't a teenage boy. He was a man who had dealt with pain and loss. A man who most likely didn't make any overture without a lot of thought and without a lot of consideration.

She poured herself a bowl of soup then sat down in the last empty chair. Right beside Silas.

As she ate, she felt Silas's eyes on her.

"So, Josie, you still doing that kid thing?" Hal asked, balancing his chair on its two back legs.

"I'm doing the after-school program. Yes."

"You were always better at the after-school stuff than the school stuff, weren't you?" Hal laughed at his own lame joke. Josie chose to ignore him.

"You know what they used to call her in school, Silas?"

"I don't think I'm interested," Silas said quietly.

Hal rocked his chair back and forth, his gaze flicking

between Josie and Silas. "Back then she was 'Raising Cane.' And could she ever."

Don't let him get to you, Josie reminded herself. *He's rude and obnoxious and you've gotten past that.*

"Yeah, our Josie here could party with the best of 'em. Actually, she was the best of 'em." Hal dropped his chair down with a *thunk* and leaned forward, his soup bowl between his hands. "Remember the time you and Arlan took his truck right down Main Street? You were standing in the back, in the truck box, three sheets to the wind, laughing and yelling. I couldn't believe you didn't get arrested." Hal shook his head as if he still couldn't believe it. "Or get sick. Yeah, our Josie had quite the enviable constitution. Could party hearty until dawn, then show up at school the next day, fresh as a daisy." Hal got up and put his soup bowl down. "You tangle with Raising Cane and you'll get more than you bargained for, Marstow."

Josie's face grew hot with mortification.

Why was Hal doing this? What could he possibly stand to gain by dredging up her past?

Josie kept her gaze down as she got to her feet and put the bowl on the table.

The walls closed in on her and her breath tangled in her throat as her past raised its murky head once more. She couldn't be here. She had to get out.

She stumbled blindly to the door, pushed it open and stepped outside. She leaned against the wall, the wood of the siding pressing into her back.

Was she doomed to have her past thrown up at her again and again? And why in front of Silas?

And why does that matter?

She didn't want to examine that thought too closely.

The door opened slowly but she didn't look over to see who it was. If it was Hal, she would go home.

"Hey, there." The quiet voice beside her made her feel

even more self-conscious. "I just came out to see how you're doing."

"Raising Cane is just fine, thanks." She didn't mean for the bitter note to slip into her voice. And why did she feel her throat thickening with tears? What Hal said she had heard before.

But hearing him say it in front of Silas bothered her more than she cared to analyze.

"Hal talks too much."

"That's been established." Josie hugged herself against the chill from the fall breeze sifting around them, bringing with it the promise of colder weather.

Winter was coming and she was still in High Plains. Not where she imagined herself to be when she was sending out résumés a scant seven months ago. Her dreams and plans had been as tossed about by the tornado as her house had been.

"Don't let it bother you," Silas said. "What he was talking about was all in the past. What he was saying, that's not who you are now."

Josie dropped her head against the wall. "People in this town have long memories." She drew in a long, slow breath, willing the tears away. "It's like no one wants me to forget who I once was."

Silas kept his gaze ahead. What was going through his mind? He'd had his doubts in the beginning about her ability to take care of his daughter, surely he had even more now? Silas had his own problems, his own ghosts haunting his life. The ghost of his perfect, unsullied wife.

"I guess that's part of the problem of living in a small town," Silas said. "The past keeps coming back."

Josie sighed. "Again and again. I feel like every day I've got to atone for something I did to someone, somewhere."

Silas frowned. "What could you possibly have done to Hal?"

"Go to a party with him, but leave with another guy.

Refuse to bootleg for him when I turned twenty-one and he was a few months shy. And assorted other grievances."

"And you still remember?" Silas's quiet question had a tinge of reprimand to it. "I think forgetting it would be healthier. Put it behind you. Move on."

"If I don't remember, someone else will. And it isn't so bad to remember. I've hurt people. Done some pretty lousy things and, well, I don't want to make the same mistakes again."

"This is where I'm getting confused." Silas crossed his arms over his chest and leaned against the wall beside her. "I remember hearing in church that grace was free. Doesn't God put our sins behind us once we've confessed them?"

"Now you're preaching to me about God?" Josie's voice held a touch of irony but at the same time, she felt a surge of hope. The anger wasn't in his voice anymore. Was he getting over his wife's death?

Silas shrugged. "I have my grievances with God, but that doesn't mean you have to." He turned to her. "And you didn't answer my question."

In the distance, the river flowed, the sunlight dancing off the tips of the waves, sending out flashes of light. Life kept going. She knew that and yet…

"To answer your question, yes, God forgives us. And He remembers our sins no more. I know that, but tell that to my grandmother."

"No," Silas said, turning to her. "I'm telling it to you. Your grandmother seems to have her own problems, but you shouldn't make them yours."

The concern in his voice called to her and as their eyes met and clung, she felt it again. That arc of awareness almost as real as a touch.

"Why does this matter to you, Silas?"

"I'm not sure. Why does it matter to you how I deal with Kelly's death?"

She couldn't answer him, either. She just knew she cared about him. And that she was attracted to him.

And that both were dangerous.

But the longing in his gaze negated her sane and sober reasons. The way her heart beat with yearning.

This was foolish. This was wrong.

But the sane part of her mind was extinguished by his closeness, and by the loneliness she'd experienced the past few years. A loneliness she knew she was trying to fill with busyness. With decisions.

Now Silas stood in front of her and she didn't feel lonely around him. Didn't feel that panicky sense that nothing was right in her world.

For the first time in years she felt as if the ground below her was firm, as if all the things that had happened the past few months had brought her to this moment.

He moved a bit closer and suddenly his hand was on her waist, hers on his. His face grew unfocused as it drew near.

She closed her eyes, seeking sanity, clinging to reality, not the dream in front of her.

He misses his wife. He hasn't fully grieved her death. Kelly was perfect.

And Josie wasn't her.

She pulled away before both of them did something truly foolish. Something both of them would regret.

She had her plans, he had his baggage.

Best leave things as they were.

Chapter Eleven

The day was over.

Silas leaned back in his chair watching the sun slip behind the horizon. He'd been working all evening, trying to get caught up on the ranch work he'd had to put off when he was working in town.

He pulled his hand over his face, his callused palms rasping over the stubble on his face.

And he thought again of that almost-moment between him and Josie. The moment that she, thankfully, cut off.

He blew out his breath and leaned forward, resting his elbows on his dusty blue jeans, his bleary eyes on the darkening sky. What had he been thinking, giving her advice like that. Then, coming so close to kissing her?

The loneliness that sent him out here every night, staring at a sunset he used to share with Kelly, had made him draw nearer to Josie, had made him step over a barrier he had put up when he buried his wife more than two years ago.

Working at the Old Town Hall had tugged at that barrier and resurrected memories, but in the rebuilding, he felt as if he was participating in something important. As if he was given a chance to create new memories.

And it seemed some of those new memories included Josie Cane.

Josie was slowly making herself important to him, moving into a part of his life he hadn't shared with anyone for two years.

Scary thought.

Yet, when he thought of the conversations they had shared, how she had challenged him and encouraged him, he knew he had found someone whom he could admire.

In spite of how she clung to the past.

The click of a door behind him made him jump.

Lily stood in the doorway, one bare foot covering the other, her hair a tangle of curls.

"I thought I told you to brush your hair before you went to bed," he said, then immediately regretted his sharp tone. He knew he was just trying to cover up for the feelings swirling through his mind and that, he was sure, were as evident on his face as the sun was in the sky.

Lily simply shrugged his comment aside as of less consequence than a fly buzzing around her head. "Are you lonely, Daddy?" she asked.

Nothing like getting straight to the point.

"I've got you, punkin'," he said, evading her blunt question.

She walked across the wooden deck, her feet whispering over the boards. "But sometimes you need more than me, don't you?"

"Maybe." He brushed her unruly hair away from her face. "What's on your mind, Lily?"

Lily fiddled with the ribbon on the yoke of her nightgown, her fingers folding and unfolding it. "I feel bad that we had supper at Ms. Josie's place. And we never asked her to come over here."

"It's harder for her to come here. And that's just the way it worked out."

Why did that seem so long ago? He had traversed a lot of territory since that evening. Had gotten to know Josie in a much different way.

He had gone to dark places and had returned different. Changed, maybe.

"Could she and Alyssa come over here for supper sometime? So we can pay them back?"

He tried to picture it. Couldn't. "That's a nice idea, but I don't think it would work. You know I don't cook real good."

"We could have a hot dog roast."

"I don't know if they would like that, punkin'." He thought again of the meal Josie had prepared—and that after a day of working and volunteering wherever she felt she had to help out.

Hot dog roasts were a last-ditch meal for him. Something he threw together at six-thirty when he realized he hadn't taken any meat out for dinner.

Lily did a slow twirl in her nightgown, as if she enjoyed the way the material flowed around her ankles. The nightgown he didn't think Lily would like, but Josie had insisted on.

Now as he watched how she ran the ribbon of her nightgown through her fingers, how she fingered the material, he realized Josie had been right and that she knew his own daughter better than he did. The thought was comforting and a bit frightening.

"Alyssa said they never have hot dog roasts," Lily was saying.

"I'm sure they don't," Silas agreed, unsure of what to say to keep her at bay. If he made too much of her request, she would take it as a yes, if he put her off, she would keep going until he either gave in, or got angry.

Lily frowned at him, then leaned on the wooden arm of his chair. "I love you, Daddy."

Her sudden about-face confused him. He had no idea

where she was going, and he supposed that was her plan. However, he had to follow to see where this led. "I love you, too, punkin'."

"And you know I miss Mommy," she added, a light hitch to her voice.

"I know, honey." He stroked her hair, his own sorrow coloring his voice.

Lily sniffed, her head down. "Sometimes I wish I had a mommy again."

Silas was helpless in the face of her sadness, as he knew he would be. For a moment he wished he had never listened to Josie, had never allowed even one scrap of memory to intrude on the life he and Lily had forged.

Since that night in his daughter's bedroom, the pain came quicker and yet, each time he gave in, he felt cleansed. Whole. As if each time he lanced a sore and each time it hurt less.

But it still hurt.

"So can Josie and Alyssa come over?" She looked up at him, her eyes wide, her mouth in an exaggerated pout.

Something about her forced-cute expression triggered a comment Josie had made that day when he came to pick up Lily from the after-school program.

Matchmaking?

He couldn't imagine Lily indulging in something as adult as that. That kind of precociousness was only written into movie scripts with cute young girls as the leads.

Like Lily and Alyssa.

Lily leaned closer, her hands clasped in front of her, her delicate eyebrows scrunched in an expression of pleading, her lower lip quivering just a bit. "Please, Daddy? It would be so fun and I can show Alyssa my kitties and the cows and my secret hideout. She said she doesn't have her own secret hideout and really wants to see mine."

Don't give in, she's just messing with your head.

But even as he caught his daughter's hangdog expression, he imagined himself showing Josie around the ranch. He remembered the rapt look on her face when they were driving to Manhattan. How much she enjoyed the wide-open spaces of the fields.

She would love the ranch.

"But Ms. Cane has to find someone to take care of her grandmother. How would she do that?" He was grasping at straws here, but he felt he had to put up some kind of resistance.

"Ms. Josie has lots of friends who can help. Like her friend Ms. Appleton. I heard Ms. Appleton tell Ms. Josie that she thought you were cute. I didn't hear what Ms. Josie said. Something about little pitchers and big ears."

Silas's neck warmed at the thought that Nicki and Josie were discussing him.

"I don't know, honey."

"I can ask her, Daddy. Then you don't have to." Lily leaned closer. "Please, Daddy. I want to have my friend here."

Silas shook his head, even as his resolve wavered. Not that he was so resolved. Spending time with Josie wasn't difficult to imagine. Really.

"Okay." He drew the world out slowly, to let her know that his concession had been hard-won. "You can ask her. But it won't be anything fancy. Just hot dogs, remember." Even as he spoke the words, second thoughts attacked him, but he couldn't back down now.

"Yippee." Lily did another twirl, then grabbed Silas around the neck, hugging him tightly. "You're the bestest daddy," she said. She planted a noisy kiss on his cheek and pulled back, her eyes boring into his. "We can ask her when we go to church on Sunday."

"Whoa. I didn't agree to church." Sure, he'd had his moment of prayer. Sure, he'd declared a kind of truce in his anger toward God, but that's all it was. Working on the Old Town Hall had been his way of telling God that things were getting a bit better.

But church?

In a community like High Plains, going to church moved things up to a more public level. And gave people a chance to ask him how he was doing. To tell him they would pray for him. That they were praying for him.

Just like they did at Kelly's funeral.

He didn't know if he was ready for that kind of in-your-face faith.

"But how will we get them to come?" Lily was asking. "I have a new dress that I want to wear sooo, sooo bad. And then I can go to Sunday school and hear the rest of the story. The teacher said we would finish it this week. You can wear your nice shirt again and we can sit together in church before Sunday school. Like we always used to. And I miss church, Daddy. I like going."

Silas felt as if he was floundering and yet, even as his daughter laid out her obviously well-thought-out arguments and even as he tried to refute them, more memories intruded.

Memories of sitting in church with Kelly on one side, Lily on the other. Him and his girls.

Reading the Bible, listening to the message and singing the songs. Being with God's people and worshipping Him.

He allowed the memory to rise up and settle in his mind. The pain came along with, but it didn't hurt as much. He had been at odds with God since his wife died. Could he go again? Did God deserve his worship?

God didn't take your wife away. Cancer did.

As Josie's words slipped into his consciousness, Silas's perceptions of his faith shifted once again. Deep in his heart he knew Josie was right.

Then Silas looked at his young daughter and saw the shining light in her eyes. He knew he didn't want to be the one to extinguish it. He may have his own issues with God, but he didn't think it was right to make that decision for his daughter.

"Okay, honey. We'll ask Josie when we go to church on Sunday."

"Yay." Lily hugged him again, kissed him again. "Can you come up with me and tuck me in like Mommy used to?"

"Sure. I guess."

As he followed his daughter up to her room, he wondered if he had done the right thing in agreeing to go to church.

As she settled into bed, the smile on her face sealed the deal for him. He hadn't exactly been hitting them out of the park where Lily was concerned. To do this one thing for her wasn't hard, even though another part of him wagged a warning finger.

He ignored the other part of him. Because, whether he wanted to admit it straight out or not, hiding behind Lily's request gave him a good opportunity to ask Josie over. It was that thought that created an unexpected frisson of anticipation.

She pulled the blankets up to her chin and snuggled down into bed.

"Daddy," she asked, "can you tell me a story? About Mommy?"

Silas looked down at his little girl and thought of the tears she had shed the last time he'd talked about Kelly. He didn't want her to feel that pain again.

"I don't know any stories, honey," he said.

Lily held his gaze, a hurt expression on her face.

"But, Daddy—"

Silas bent over and dropped a quick kiss on her forehead. "Just go to sleep, honey. There's a good girl."

She nodded and turned away.

He felt a bit guilty, but he had done the right thing. Talking about Kelly hurt, but he was an adult. He could deal with the pain.

He was saving her from a lot of hurt, he reminded himself as he closed the door on his daughter's bedroom.

He didn't want her to have to go through the storm he had endured only a few days ago. He couldn't bear it.

"No more doughnuts, Kasey." Nicki softened her admonishment with a gentle smile as she took the doughnut from the little girl. She put it back in the box sitting on the blanket she and Josie had spread out on the grass of the park.

"Lunch will be in an hour," Josie said. "Can you wait until then?"

Kasey started to whine and screwed up her face in what seemed to be an attempt to garner sympathy from her foster mom as she rubbed her stomach.

Nicki glanced at Josie who was trying hard not to laugh. "Your tummy will be happier if you don't fill it up before we have lunch, okay?"

Kasey looked at Josie, who glanced away, keeping her gaze focused on the river running along the park. It was so hard to look into those sad eyes and not let pity take over good sense.

Ever since the little girl was found wandering along the riverbank after the tornado, public sympathy had run high for the little tyke. Josie, best friend of Nicki who had taken Kasey in, knew better than most the trauma the little girl was still dealing with.

Kasey heaved another theatrical sigh, but then toddled over the grass to where Alyssa was sitting on another blanket, setting out some dolls for Kasey to play with.

"Does she still wake up at night?" Josie asked, pitching her voice low so the little girl couldn't hear as she put the rest of the doughnuts back in the picnic cooler she had packed that morning.

Nicki pulled her long legs up to her chest and wrapped her arms around them. "Not as much as she used to, but she still has moments that her face goes blank and I know her mind is slipping back to that day."

"I am so surprised we haven't heard anything. About her mother."

"I know. I hate to think that somewhere her mother is looking for her, scared and afraid, but at the same time, I'm getting so attached to Kasey. Her story just pulls at my heart." Nicki's eyes followed Kasey as she and Alyssa played with the dolls.

Josie plucked a blade of grass and toyed with it. "There's so many sad stories, aren't there? This tornado has hurt more than buildings."

Nicki nodded. "Jesse Logan is still struggling with the death of his wife. Can't imagine all that he's had to deal with because of that. Now he's trying to figure out how to take care of his little girls."

"Which makes me think of Clay. Have you heard anything from him?"

Nicki's eyes took on a faraway look and then she shook her head again. "Clay is in the past, Josie. I prefer to leave him there."

"The past has a way of sneaking up on you when you least expect it," Josie said with a hint of melancholy.

Her own mind cast back to what she and Silas had spoken of a few days ago. Her eyes flicked over her shoulder, past the park they were sitting in to the Old Town Hall.

She was surprised to see Silas was working on a Saturday. What had he done with Lily?

She hadn't signed up for today, but suddenly she wanted to be at the hall. To see him face-to-face. To test this new thing she sensed had sprung up between them.

Part of her felt she was crazy to read more into his touch than mere comfort yet she knew someone like Silas did nothing without thinking the implications of it through to the end.

And what are the implications for you?

Josie stilled the question. Goodness knows she had enough voices chattering around in her head. Voices that accused, condemned, wondered and questioned each action and each motive.

The door of the Old Town Hall opened and a man stepped out carrying an armload of scrap lumber. He tossed it into a trailer, then turned and stopped.

Even across this distance she felt Silas's eyes zero in on her.

And she couldn't look away.

"You're looking pensive," Nicki teased her, nudging Josie with her elbow. Then she caught the direction of Josie's gaze and glanced back herself. "Well, well, well," she said softly. "And once again I catch you staring at the very handsome and single Silas Marstow. Very interesting."

"You know those workers are really coming along on the hall," Josie said with an airy tone. "I think it might even get done on time."

"Oh, very good try," Nicki said with a throaty laugh, glancing over her shoulder again. "So. Silas Marstow. We've talked about him before."

"*You've* talked about him before," Josie returned.

"He's good-looking. Single."

"Widowed, with a little girl and a whole lot of baggage."

"That you could help him unload, I'm sure," Nicki teased.

"I've got enough of my own." Josie turned her attention back to the cooler. "I'm sure the girls would want a juice box right now."

"Probably. But I think there's something way more juicy going on right under my nose."

Josie shot an irritated frown at her friend. "Nothing's happening. He's just…" She knew her friend well enough to stop there. When Nicki found out Josie was making plans to leave High Plains, she promised she would find a way to put a stop to her plans. If she had any inkling of Josie's still tenuous emotions, she would be fanning that particular ember with an ardor that Josie was helpless to stop.

"He's just a friend." Nicki finished Josie's statement, a world of meaning in her gentle voice. "You sound like a movie star pretending to ignore what everyone else can see."

Josie chose to ignore what her friend was saying. She opened the lid of the cooler and was about to pull out a couple of juice boxes for the girls when a voice called out Nicki's name.

It was the urgency in the voice that caught Josie's attention. That and the fact that the voice belonged to Colt Ridgeway, the town sheriff.

Both girls turned as Colt strode toward them, his long legs eating up the distance in seconds. His car, parked along the main street, added a note of somberness to the moment.

Josie couldn't stop the flip of her heart at the sight of his uniform. She had a long history with policemen. Not Colt, thank goodness. However, every time she saw him, she wondered if he knew of her record at High Plains's detachment.

Colt stopped in front of them, his hands on his hips, the butt of his handgun brushing his fingertips, all of which served to underline his position in the town.

"I need to talk to you, Nicki." He glanced past Nicki to Kasey, then dropped to one knee beside the women. "It's about Kasey."

Nicki's hand flew to her chest, as if preparing for whatever news Colt might deliver. Josie moved close to her friend, putting her arm around her to support her.

Colt's blue eyes flicked from Josie to Nicki. "I'm on my way to talk to a woman who claims to be Kasey's mother."

"Again?" Nicki asked. Josie squeezed her friend's shoulder.

"Maybe this will be a false alarm, as well," Josie assured Nicki, shooting Colt a questioning glance.

Colt shrugged. "It might be a scam, it might be the real deal. But I thought you should know."

Nicki nodded, but Josie saw her expression go numb.

Colt looked like he wanted to say more, then he pushed himself to his feet. "Sorry. I thought I'd keep you informed as things happen. I'll let you know the minute I find anything out one way or the other."

He gave Nicki a sympathetic smile, then left.

As Colt walked away, Josie saw Nicki's hand snake up to brush the tears sliding down her cheeks.

"Hello, Mr. Marstow," Alyssa called out as Josie handed her friend a tissue.

Josie shot a quick glance past Nicki just as Silas came to a stop in front of them. He held a cooking pot in his hands.

"Hey, Nicki. Josie." He glanced over at Colt's vehicle, then at Josie. "You're not working at the Old Town Hall today?" he asked Josie.

She shook her head then recognized her soup pot.

"I saw you sitting here and Reverend Michael asked me to give you your soup pot."

How helpful, Josie thought as she held her hand out for the pot, wondering if Reverend Michael, still feeling flush with his matchmaking success with Colt and Lexi, was trying his hand at it again. There was no reason for Silas to give her the pot now.

"Thank you," she said, feeling suddenly self-conscious as she set the pot beside the cooler.

Too easily she recalled the feel of his hand on her hip, his nearness and she was afraid that if she were to look up at him, she would blush. Again.

"Howdy, Mr. Marstow. Where's Lily?" Alyssa called out.

"She's staying at a neighbor's today," Silas said with a smile for the little girl.

"You should have taken her along. She could help me play with Kasey."

"Don't you see enough of her?" Silas teased.

"No. She's my bestest friend."

The light smile curving his lips was as much of a surprise as his gentle teasing of Alyssa was. Then he turned back to them, his smile fading away as his gaze snagged Josie's.

"What did Colt want?" Silas asked, jerking his thumb over his shoulder toward the police car pulling away from the curb.

Josie shot a quick glance over her shoulder. Kasey and Alyssa were playing with their dolls, but she lowered her voice nonetheless. "He came to tell us that he was on his way to talk to a woman who may or may not be Kasey's mother."

Nicki drew in a shuddering breath. "Sorry," she muttered, digging in her pocket for a hanky. "I knew this would happen."

Silas was quiet and this time Josie took a chance and glanced up at him. He towered above them, his expression somber.

"A dangerous by-product of caring." The cynical note in his voice made Josie's heart drop.

Was he referring to his wife? The pain she felt surprised her as much as his unexpected statement.

"That may be true," Nicki said. "But how else can I take care of the children I do? I think it's still better to give love where and when you can."

"As long as you know that with giving comes the potential for a lot of hurt."

With that enigmatic remark, Silas turned and left.

Josie watched him go, the pain she felt at his earlier remark intensified. He was talking about his wife.

She should pull back while her heart was still whole. Keep as aloof as Silas seemed to.

Kasey presented her foot with its loose shoelace to Nicki who bent her head, focusing on the immediate needs of the little girl.

The afternoon slipped by but Josie noticed Nicki's distraction. Her eyes constantly slid to the street, as if waiting for Colt. Each time a car slowed down, Nicki jumped. Josie's heart ached for her friend and for what she might have to give up.

A flash of sunlight reflected off glass caught her eye and both she and Nicki turned at the same time. Colt's car pulled up to the curb and as he got out, Josie's heart was thrumming in her throat.

Without looking at her friend, she reached over and grabbed Nicki's hand. Together they stood, as if to face whatever news Colt might have on their feet.

The smile on his face said it all. As he came nearer he was shaking his head.

"And?" Nicki asked, her voice a thin sound.

"False alarm." Colt's smile grew.

Nicki wavered as she pressed her hand to her chest.

"I'm glad and yet…" Nicki glanced over her shoulder at Kasey.

"Thought you'd like to know as soon as possible." Colt's radio squawked and he poked his thumb over his shoulder. "Gotta get going. I got another call." As he walked away, he started talking into his radio.

Josie willed her pounding heart to quit as she supported her friend.

"That was a close call," Nicki said, hugging herself, drawing in a shaky breath.

"I wonder if they'll ever find her mother," Josie murmured.

"For now, my focus is Kasey," Nicki said quietly. "And what I can give her."

"Even if it hurts?" Silas's comment slid into her mind.

"Even if it hurts." Nicki gently pulled away from Josie and walked over to Kasey.

As Josie watched her friend kneel down beside the little

girl, she wondered if love had the potential to cause pain as Silas said.

Her feelings for Silas were changing, which had the potential to cause hurt for her, as well. But should she shield her heart? Take a chance on Silas?

Change her plans? Plans that had already been changed so many times?

And what would you do instead?

And did Silas even care for her?

Chapter Twelve

Silas sat back in the pew and allowed his gaze to travel around the church. The morning chill inside the building, the sound of the organ playing quietly in the background, the sense of waiting in the air was achingly familiar.

Light from the sun poured through the stained-glass windows, lending an air of reverence to the moment.

The last time he'd been inside this building was at Kelly's funeral. He tried to pull out the memories of that day but all that came to mind was fragments. The organist playing "Nearer My God to Thee." The spray of tiger lilies on the coffin, Kelly's favorite flowers.

The thought that Kelly's fight on earth was done and that she was now nearer to God than she'd been on earth. And definitely nearer to God than Silas had felt.

As the bits and pieces slipped like a montage through his mind, he felt pain. But the pain wasn't as harsh as it used to be and didn't cut as jaggedly.

The church was filling up and his eyes flicked over the congregation again. Looking for Josie.

That was just so he could find her afterward, he reminded himself, picking up the bulletin again. He scanned the contents and then a movement in the aisle beside him caught his eye.

A woman. Tall, slender, silky blond hair hanging past her shoulders. She wore an orange dress with some kind of sweater on top.

And she was pushing a wheelchair, with a young girl walking alongside.

Silas followed Josie's progress down the aisle. She stopped a few pews ahead, then fussed with her grandmother, as if making sure she was settled in.

Then as she straightened, she looked back.

Their gazes locked for a beat, and as a slow smile crept across her mouth, he felt an answering tug of attraction.

And he smiled back.

She sat down and as the rest of the church filled up, Silas found his attention returning to Josie again and again.

Reverend Michael got up and announced the first song and Silas had to grin at the sight of the minister all dressed up. The last time he'd seen him, he had a rip in his blue jeans, sawdust in his hair and a five o'clock shadow.

But the welcoming smile was the same, and Silas felt himself relax.

As he listened to Reverend Garrison lead them through the worship service, he was glad Kelly's parents had insisted that the minister from their old church do the funeral. At the time, he'd been upset, but now he was thankful it had gone that way. Bad enough that the church held memories of Kelly, he didn't have to associate Michael Garrison with those memories, as well.

Reverend Michael then announced that the children were dismissed for Sunday school.

Lily scooted out of the pew and went directly to Alyssa. She whispered something in her friend's ear, then they both looked back at Silas, then they giggled and flounced up to the front of the church.

Silas didn't even want to speculate what that was about.

When the last giggles dissipated and the door to the downstairs was closed, Michael picked up his Bible.

"Today we're looking at Joshua 4," he announced. "That's at the front of the Bible for those of you who don't know your way around."

Silas folded his arms over his chest and sat back, not bothering to look up the passage. He was just waiting to see what Reverend Michael was going to preach about. Hoping it wasn't some overly sugary sermon about how the people of God are always happy and that if you're not, there's something wrong with your faith.

Because right now, he wasn't there.

But as Reverend Garrison read, Silas's eyes flicked to Josie who was holding the Bible out for her grandmother. Josie's head was bent as she followed along. The sun through the window shone off her hair.

She reached up and casually tucked a bit of it behind her ear, revealing her profile.

Josie had been a pretty girl in high school; that much he'd seen from the pictures in the photo album. How many boyfriends did she have in high school? How rough was her past?

Bad enough that she thought she needed to atone for it. Bad enough that she was here in church, holding the Bible for a grandmother who criticized her at every turn.

Why did Josie stick around? Why she let people get to her the way they did?

He reined in his thoughts, forcing his attention back to Reverend Garrison. He was here, the least he could do was listen.

Besides, if Reverend Michael was working on restoring the Old Town Hall, maybe it would be best if Silas had an inkling of what he was talking about. Just in case it came up in conversation.

"…we are people who live in community, who live in relationship and an important part of that community is the sharing of story. That's why we look forward to Founders' Day. To recreate the stories that brought us to where we are." Silas felt a momentary stab of familiar pain as another memory of Kelly came to mind. How she had hoped she would be around for Founders' Day. How she wanted to be a part of the story of the community.

"...that's why we put up monuments," Reverend Garrison was saying. "I believe it's not only to celebrate what happened at that time, but to serve as a reminder, much like the stones Joshua told the people to put up did. It created an opportunity for people of the community to tell the children the stories of God's faithfulness. To tell the current and next generation of how God has worked in our lives. To tell our stories. And to tell our stories for God's glory, not ours. The stones become a place for dialogue. For memories. To create questions. When your children ask...we need to tell them the stories they want to hear. We need to tell them that God has worked in our lives. Some of the stories we have to share are sad. Each of us here has lost something in the recent tornado and has lost something even before that." Reverend Michael's gaze ticked over many of the people in the congregation, as if acknowledging that pain.

Silas felt as if he was looking deeply into his own soul and dragging out the very stories Silas had tried to bury.

"Each of us here has pains and burdens to bear. But we need to talk about our stories, to share them within community, within family. So that we can show how God has brought us through to the other side. And alternately, what we are dealing with right now. Because to share our stories, to share our sorrow, is also part of living in community."

Reverend Garrison's words dived into Silas's heart as he remembered Lily asking him to tell her stories of Kelly. He had refused.

But if, according to Reverend Garrison, the point was to show how God had carried him through that time, then it was probably a good thing he hadn't said anything to Lily. Because to explore the past was to expose his lack of trust in God.

What about that moment? In the bedroom? When you felt God's presence?

And what about your parents? What about their own love for the Lord? A love that they instilled in you? At one time you and God were close. Surely you can't discount that?

The growing voice wove in and out, alternately making him feel guilty and, peculiarly, making him see the emptiness that had filled his life the past two years.

Silas folded his arms over his chest but he couldn't block out Michael Garrison's words. When the congregation stood for the final song, he felt as if God was nudging at him, reminding him of the relationship they once had.

The words of the last song, "Parents Tell Your Children," reminded him again of his parents. Of the legacy of faith they had passed on to him. A legacy he had pushed aside.

God didn't kill your wife. Cancer did.

Those particularly telling words slipped back into his mind just as Josie walked past him, pushing her grandmother in her wheelchair. Her friend Nicki Appleton was walking alongside her.

But Josie glanced at him as she passed and gave him a careful smile. "Good to see you here," she said.

"It was Lily's idea to attend." He fell into step and decided to get straight to the point, trying to push out Reverend Garrison's haunting words. "Lily has a few other ideas. One of which is to have you over. For supper tonight. She wants to pay you back for the time you had us over. A Marstow always pays his or her debts, so I thought it was a good idea, as well."

Josie's grin was a pleasant surprise. Then she glanced down at her grandmother and Silas easily read her hesitation and the reason for it.

"Mrs. Carter, you're welcome to come, as well," Silas offered.

Betty Carter shot him a querulous look. "I can't go out at night. Too much pain. And Josie should stay home. Take care of her responsibilities."

"But Alyssa is invited, as well," Silas said, deliberately misreading Betty's meaning.

"That little girl has too many people catering to her. She's becoming less like her mother every day and more like her aunt." Betty's mouth pulled into a tight circle showing her disapproval.

Silas caught a hint of sorrow in Josie's eyes and once again he felt sorry for her. Living with Betty both when she was young, and now while they were waiting for their lives to get back on track, must have been tremendously hard on her self-esteem.

"You can be happy about that," Silas said as they walked through the back door. "Josie is a good person."

This netted him a harrumph. "I could tell you stories, mister. She's nothing like your Kelly."

Silas was surprised that the way Betty talked about Josie bothered him more than the reference to his wife did.

Silas turned to Josie. "Is there any way you could come? I know Lily won't stop bothering me until you do."

Josie glanced down at her grandmother "I'd love to, but…" Her voice trailed off.

Was he imagining the regret in her voice and in that sidelong glance she gave him?

"You better stay home, missy." Betty Carter's tone implied that Josie would do nothing less than what she ordered.

They were through the back entrance of the church and in the foyer.

"Gramma, do you mind waiting here a minute?" Josie asked, moving her grandmother to one side of the foyer. "I have to pick up Alyssa. You'll be okay here?"

"Oh, sure. Just park me here by the coatrack. I'll be fine." Betty waved her granddaughter off with an imperious gesture that implied anything but.

"I'll keep your grandmother company if you don't mind getting Lily for me," Silas said.

Josie shot him a look of pure relief. "Gladly done." She turned and left, the skirt of her orange dress flowing around her tanned legs.

Silas glanced down at Betty, a peculiar expression on her face as she watched her granddaughter leave. He wanted to say something to Betty, but, to be honest, she was a bit intimidating.

"She's a pretty girl, my granddaughter," Betty said suddenly.

"That she is." On this, at least, they could agree.

"Take my advice. Stay away from her."

Silas felt a burst of anger. He was about to say something more when a couple stopped and greeted him by name and welcomed him to the church service.

While they chatted, a few more people stopped to say hello and welcome him back. The lost lamb back to the fold. He was surprised to know that people missed him. He and Kelly hadn't lived there very long, but it seemed they had become a part of the community nonetheless.

While they were talking, Betty wheeled herself away from him. Just as well. The more time he spent with her the more tempted he was to interfere. He shouldn't get involved. Josie was simply the teacher of his daughter and a somewhat friend whom he owed a favor.

Who was he kidding, he thought as Josie came back up the stairs. Lily held one hand, Alyssa the other.

The picture looked so right. Josie flanked by the two girls who could easily be sisters. They fit, he thought as a shiver danced down his spine. Then Josie's gaze caught his and a peculiar sensation welled up in his chest. Something he hadn't felt in a long time. A sense of family and togetherness.

Lily let go of Josie's hand and ran toward him. "They're coming. Ms. Appleton said she would Gramma-sit so Ms. Cane and Alyssa can come."

Silas tore his gaze away from Josie. "Gramma-sit?" he asked his daughter.

"She's not a baby so Ms. Appleton can't hardly be baby-sitting, can she?"

"Not hardly," Silas agreed. He looked up at Josie standing in front of him. "I'm glad you can come. It's a causal affair, so wear blue jeans. It won't be anything fancy, but there will be food of one form or another."

"Food sounds good," Josie said, her voice holding a hint of laughter. "If you want I can bring dessert."

"No. No," Lily protested. "We always have s'mores when we have a hot dog roast."

"That sounds even better," Josie said. She gave Silas another smile. "I'll see you tonight then."

This was a mistake. This was a mistake. The words pounded through Josie's head in time to her and Alyssa's footsteps going up Silas's walk to his farmhouse.

Lily and Alyssa had announced Josie and Alyssa's visit as a matter of course and had conveniently done so in front of Nicki.

Who had immediately offered to take care of Josie's grandmother. Josie had tried to protest, but her friend seemed to think Josie deserved a night off.

Josie felt pushed, but at the same time a part of her was drawn to the idea of spending time with Silas on his farm. So now she was here.

She lifted her hand to knock on the door, when a voice called out to her.

"We're over here," Lily called out. Josie looked around

and saw the little girl just past the house, standing beside a large red barn.

Josie caught the scent of smoke, and remembered Silas saying something about a hot dog roast. Alyssa, spotting her friend, ran ahead of Josie. The two girls grabbed each other in a big hug, and jumped around squealing, as if they hadn't seen each other for weeks instead of hours.

Josie highly suspected the two girls had much to do with the arrangements of this evening.

But you didn't mind coming, a small voice reminded her.

Josie shoved her hands in the front pockets of her blue jeans, thankful she had decided at the last minute to throw a fleece hoodie over her shirt. There was a distinct chill in the air. Snow could come any day. The thought sent a shiver of depression through Josie.

She came around the corner of the barn and spied Silas feeding a few sticks of wood into a fire crackling in a cement-enclosed fire pit. A wooden table, covered with a tablecloth, held hot dogs and buns, and various condiments.

Silas stood as she came near, brushing his hands over his pants. His smile banished her misgivings and summoned a frisson of awareness. "Glad you made it," he said, handing her a hot-dog stick.

A few moments later she held a hot dog over the fire, turning it every so often, as Lily had shown her, so it wouldn't burn. Alyssa was preparing a hot dog bun.

"I didn't realize there was a method to cooking these things properly," Josie said, flashing a grin at Silas.

"Hot dog cooking is an underrated art," Silas said, pouring ketchup over his. "Lily and I have gotten pretty good at it. And these aren't just ordinary run-of-the-mill hot dogs. I had these sausages specially made."

Josie slipped the cooked hot dog in the bun and accepted a plate with salad on it from Alyssa. Then she sat back in the lawn chair that Silas had provided for her, and took her first bite.

As she chewed she shot Silas a startled glance. "That is absolutely delicious," she said wiping the ketchup off her mouth with a napkin. "I've had hot dogs before, but nothing like this."

"I'm glad I could offer you a whole new culinary experience," Silas said, wiping his own mouth.

The girls had already finished their first hot dog, and were poking fat, white marshmallows on the roasting forks. "You put the chocolate on the graham squares," Lily ordered Alyssa as she carefully turned the marshmallows.

"What are you doing now?" Josie asked, after she swallowed another bite of her hot dog.

Lily shot her a puzzled frown. "We're making s'mores. Haven't you ever heard of them?"

"I have, but never seen them." As Josie ate, she watched the procedure with interest.

Lily laid the soft, roasted marshmallow on the chocolate and the graham square, then sandwiched it with another graham square and carefully pulled the marshmallow off the fork.

She held the sticky business up in the air to show Josie. "You have to wait a little while for the hot marshmallow to melt the chocolate a little bit, and then you take a big bite." She handed it to Alyssa. "You have to be careful, because sometimes the graham squares get crumbly."

"Did you bring a wet facecloth?" Silas asked, finishing off the last of his hot dog.

"Whoops, I forgot," Lily said just as Alyssa took a bite of her s'more. The graham cracker crumbled and Alyssa ended up with marshmallow and chocolate dripping down her fingers and chin.

She giggled as she stuffed the rest of the treat into her mouth, then began licking her fingers.

"Let's go to the house," Lily said, catching her by the elbow. "You can wash your hands and face there." She turned to her father. "When we're done washing up, I'm going to show Alyssa my hideout."

"Don't wander too far," Silas said, wiping his hands on a paper napkin.

"Will they be okay?" Josie asked, finishing the last of her hot dog. She licked her fingers, enjoying her supper to the last drip of ketchup on her fingertips.

"Lily knows every square inch of this ranch, they'll be okay." Silas gave her a grin. "Can I make you a s'more?"

"They look scrumptious. Why not?" Josie stretched her legs out in front of her, letting the fire warm her feet. She laid her head back against the lawn chair, looking up at the darkening sky.

Faintly, over the cooling air, she heard the girls giggling, the faint sound of water bouncing over rocks.

And nothing else. She folded her hands over her stomach, and let her eyes flow around the wide-open spaces surrounding them.

"I feel suddenly very small," she said on a sigh.

Silas poked a couple of marshmallows on the forks, and squatted down to roast them. "It's pretty quiet out here, compared to town, but I love it."

"I can see why." She looked down at the fire, mesmerized by the dancing flames. Sparks flew upward, spiraling on the air, dancing toward the darkening sky. "It's been years since I've sat by a fire."

"Are there hot dog roasts in your past?" Silas asked with a grin.

"My grandmother and my sister never did anything like this. Never even went camping," Josie said, deliberately misunderstanding his question.

"But you have sat around a fire," Silas prompted carefully assembling a s'more for her.

"I did. In high school." Bush parties that either got out of control or were broken up by the local police.

Thankfully Silas made no reference to her admission.

"Here you go. One s'more." He handed her the treat, gave her a napkin, then sat down in the empty chair beside her. "Lily already gave you the warning, so I won't bother."

"I'm sure I can eat it without making a mess."

Silas grinned. "Physical impossibility."

"I take that as a challenge," Josie said, raising the crackers in a salute. She eyed the sweet confection, turning it this way and that.

"Don't mess with it too much," Silas warned. "Any minute now the marshmallow will be dripping down."

He was right and Josie doubted the chocolate was melted enough to take a proper bite without the cracker breaking. So she made an executive decision, and shoved the whole thing in her mouth. Now the challenge was to finish the thing, and still maintain some sense of decorum. As if that was possible.

Silas burst out laughing as she gingerly worked the s'more down. The sound of his laughter was like a balm to her soul and it gave her a curious lift.

Silas handed her a napkin and she put it in front of her mouth as she chewed.

"Okay, that's officially really good," Josie announced when she was finished.

Silas reached over and wiped a bit of marshmallow off her chin. "You'll want to wash your face," he suggested.

His hand slowed its movement; his voice grew quiet, and Josie felt as if everything around them grew still. Waiting. This close she could see the lines fanning out from his eyes. They were lighter than his face, as if he spent a lot of time squinting into the sun.

"Hey, Daddy, I found your shovel." Lily's voice broke the moment, and Josie pulled away, her heart thudding in her chest.

As Silas pulled away, she saw the girls. Lily was holding a shovel. Alyssa beside her.

And both of them wearing expressions of deep disappointment.

Ruined their little plan, Josie thought, getting up from the chair. And not a moment too soon.

"I'll just put it in the garage," Lily said, making a quick about-face.

"Lily, come back here," Silas called, but the girls had disappeared even more quickly than they had come.

Josie took the moment to pull herself together, then turned back to him. "Lily says you've been doing some work on the place," Josie said, hating the breathless tone in her voice.

"Yeah. I'll give you a tour."

"Shouldn't we clean up?" Josie glanced at the food still lying on the table, but Silas shook his head. "I'll get Lily and Alyssa to take care of it. If we find them."

Josie suspected the two girls were making themselves pretty scarce.

"I'll show you the cabins I've been working on," Silas said, walking ahead of her.

Josie followed him, thankful for the chance to let her heart go back to normal, for her heated cheeks to cool. She had come close to doing something irretrievably silly.

Not silly, natural, another voice chided. *He's an attractive man, you're a young woman. There's definitely an appeal.*

I'm not his kind of woman, Josie reminded herself as she followed Silas around the corner of the barn. He's just lonely. That's all.

"This is where I've put the cabins," Silas was saying, pointing out a group of small wooden buildings spaced along a row of trees. Two of the cabins were completed and the other two were still just a frame. Josie walked closer, intrigued by the idea.

"You would have guests staying right on the ranch?"

"I'm looking at setting up ranch holidays. Have people coming over, staying on a working ranch. Helping where they can." Silas slipped his hands into the pockets of his blue jeans and walked toward the first cabin. He walked up the wooden stairs and pulled open the door.

Josie followed him.

They stepped into the cool, dark interior of the cabin. The walls were wood, as was the vaulted ceiling and the floor. Railed stairs set against the side wall led to a loft in the peak of the roof. Below the loft, Josie guessed, were two bedrooms.

"I have to put in a kitchen counter yet. Buy a couple of wood heaters for each cabin. This one can sleep six, the other cabins, four." Silas walked to the middle of the cabin and did a slow turn, looking around as if inspecting his handiwork.

"You did all this yourself?" Josie asked, amazed at the amount of work he had put into just this cabin alone.

"I get a high school kid to come for the summer, but yeah, most of this I do myself. I've been a bit behind lately. It's been hard to get wood locally since the tornado, but one day you'll see this done." The quick smile he gave her held a promise of other visits. Tomorrows.

The look he gave her created another flutter in her chest.

"What would you do with these guests?" Josie asked as they left the first cabin.

"I have a few plans. The main one is some riding trips. Take them on a mini roundup of the cows in the fall. Get them to help with the haying in the summer. Have hot dog roasts."

"Don't forget the s'mores," Josie said, thankful she sounded so casual. So in charge of her runaway feelings. She turned her attention back to the cabin. "It would be fun to be involved with something like this. You could even do domestic kind of things, like berry picking and then making pies from the berries. Or apples, if you had an apple orchard." She flashed Silas a quick grin.

"Baking's not my thing," Silas said as they meandered away from the cabins. "As you know, grilled-cheese sandwiches and hot dog roasts are the extent of my culinary abilities." He led her through the grove of trees surrounding the cabins, their feet rustling in the fallen leaves carpeting the ground. A few brightly colored leaves still clung to the branches, but their days were numbered, Josie thought with a touch of melancholy.

Josie guessed from the sound of cattle lowing in the distance that she and Silas were headed toward the corrals.

"I think it could be fun," Josie said, imagining groups of people in the kitchen, rolling out pastry, baking. "And you could have, like, a joint dinner at the end of the holiday."

"I can see you doing that kind of thing. You seem to like feeding people."

"I like cooking. Alyssa and I did more baking when we lived in my house. It's been a bit harder lately. My grandmother is a bit fussy." Josie plucked a leaf from a tree, twirling it in her fingers.

"She's not doing so well, it seems."

Josie shook her head. "I don't know what's going on with her. The doctor is equally puzzled. Though the X-rays show that her bones are mending, she still seems to be in so much pain. The physiotherapist can't do as much with her as she'd like because of the pain."

"That ties you down quite a bit." Silas angled her a wry look.

Josie nodded, tracing the veins of the dry leaf, unwilling to let her mind go too far down that path.

"She didn't live with you before the tornado, did she?"

"No. We each had our own places."

"What if she can't walk again? Would that change your plans?"

Josie didn't want to let that thought take root. Her grandmother was a priority in her life right now, but she didn't want to think that Betty would be dependent on her for the rest of her life.

"Have you thought about putting her in an extended-care facility?" Silas asked.

Josie dropped the leaf. "I can't. I owe her too much."

"Like what?"

Josie's steps slowed. "I'm sure you know I wasn't the easiest granddaughter." She gave a short laugh. "I probably took a number of years off her life when I was a teenager. Maybe even before. I wasn't the nicest kid and I was an even worse teen."

"You were young."

"I was wild. You've heard the stories."

"But I haven't seen the evidence." Silas scratched his forehead with his finger. "I've never heard anyone say how you've hurt them. I've never heard of any property damage."

"I've kept my grandmother up at all hours worrying about me. I know what I was and I know what I did to my grandmother. Sure she's difficult, but I owe her a lot." She hugged her arms around herself. The sun was almost down and the gathering dusk brought the evening chill.

"I think you've already paid that debt, Josie." Silas's voice was quiet, but it held a note of conviction. "Don't you think you're allowed to move past that? To put that behind you?"

As they broke out of the trees, Josie shot him a puzzled glance. "You don't even know what I did. I used to go out and get drunk. I skipped school to go drink by the river. I hung around with a wild bunch—"

Silas turned to her and caught her by the shoulders. "Who cares? That was in the past. Don't you believe you've been forgiven?"

"Well, yes, but my grandmother—"

"Is mining your guilt. As long as you let your grandmother keep bringing up your past, she will have that hold over you."

"She doesn't have much of a hold over me," Josie protested.

"I think she's created a false sense of guilt and responsibility. And it seems to me you think the only way to get away from that is to leave."

Josie looked up at Silas, wondering why this mattered so much to him. "I don't know of any other way out. I can't live in the same town as her anymore. Not after spending so much time with her in my house."

Silas let his one hand drift up and down her arm. "I think you should be careful not to let her attitude toward you get in the way of your relationship with God."

Josie lifted her gaze to his and in the twilight, his eyes glittered. "Why do you care about my relationship with God?"

Silas watched his hand drifting up and down her arm in a curious gesture of comfort. "I've had my own struggles with God. I'm still working on a few things. Working a few things out." He lifted his gaze to hers. "You've encouraged me to look in the past. It's still hard, but I realized I needed to go back there. The sermon on Sunday reminded me of that."

"I was glad to see you in church. I hope that you found some peace."

"I found a lot." He gave her a gentle smile. "I got permission to go into the past and to appreciate what a gift Kelly was." He kept his hand on her arm. "I have you to thank for that." His eyes delved into hers and Josie felt a connection spring up between them.

She wanted to look away. Couldn't.

"I'm glad. I think it's healthy for you and for Lily. She needs to have permission to relive her own memories."

"So you told me." Silas's gaze intensified. "But while you told me that I was wrong in avoiding the past, I think you're wrong in spending as much time there as you do. I don't know what you were like in the past. Sure, I've heard the stories, but I know what you're like now, Josie. You're good and kind. Generous and caring. And that's all that matters to me."

He stopped and his hand tightened his grip on her arm.

Her heart stuttered and her breath seemed clogged in her throat as he spoke. Their gazes locked. Held. The air was thick with unspoken words and she read longing in his gaze. A longing that matched hers perfectly.

The moment extended and she held it carefully, as if afraid that the wrong movement, the wrong word could shatter it.

His hand moved to her shoulder and Josie put her hand over it. Anchoring him to her.

She couldn't look away, and then his face grew blurred as he moved closer again.

She closed her eyes, unable to stop her drifting toward him as at her center swirled a storm of conflicting feelings.

She shouldn't.

But she wanted to.

She tightened her grip on his hand, as if clinging to something solid.

Then his lips were on hers, his hand encircled her neck, his fingers tangled in her hair.

And the storm stilled.

When he finally pulled away, she wanted to protest, to pull him back to her.

His fingers trailed over her cheek and his eyes traveled over her face as if examining every plane.

Josie's starved heart fed on his attention, his gentle consideration.

He kissed her again. And again, his arms crushing her against his chest. She felt as if her lonely heart had finally found a resting place. As if all the plans she had lost since the tornado didn't matter anymore.

She was where she should be. In Silas's arms, resting her head on his chest.

Then, inexplicably, he drew back, lowered his hand, turned and walked away from her.

Her hands clutched her arms, as if trying to mend the breach he had created in her own defenses.

It was just a kiss, she thought, clinging to the cold reality of the words. Just a kiss. Then why did she feel as if her world had been torn apart?

Chapter Thirteen

"This doesn't look good," Lily whispered to Alyssa as she leaned against the wall of the barn. "My dad looks mad." She took a chance and peeked around the corner again, but Ms. Josie just stood on the edge of the trees, her head down.

And her dad was leaning on the corral fence, staring at the cows.

"What happened?" Alyssa whispered back, taking a peek herself.

"I don't know. They were kissing and then it looked like my dad changed his mind." Lily punched her hand against the wood of the barn. "He's so silly sometimes."

Alyssa blew out a sigh and squatted on the ground. "I give up. I don't know what to do anymore."

"We can't give up. If my daddy won't marry Josie, then who will he marry?" Lily dropped to the ground beside her friend, pulling at a clump of grass beside her. "He hasn't kissed a girl since my mom died. He was even whistling again."

"And Aunt Josie is smiling all the time." Alyssa pulled her knees up to her chest and dropped her chin on them. "We need help."

"But who's going to help us?"

"Should we pray, maybe?" Alyssa asked hesitantly.

"Is that allowed?" Lily frowned at her.

Alyssa shrugged. "I don't know. Sometimes, when we're in Manhattan, and Auntie Josie is driving, I hear her say, 'Please, Lord, let me find a parking spot,' so maybe we can pray about this."

"You'll have to help me. You're the expert. I just started going to Sunday school." Lily shot another quick look around the barn, but nothing had changed. Except Josie was walking toward them. "We have to hurry. Your aunt is coming."

Alyssa grabbed Lily's hand and scrunched her eyes closed. Lily did the same.

"Please, Lord. Let my aunt Josie and Lily's dad get together so we can be sisters." Alyssa paused and Lily opened her eyes to see if she was done, but Alyssa still had her eyes closed, so she shut hers, too. "But I know we're supposed to pray that Your will be done, so You have to do what You think is best. Amen."

Lily opened her eyes and looked back. Josie was just about here. "We should go. So your aunt doesn't think we're spying on her."

They got up and snuck through the grass to the other side of the barn.

"There you girls are."

Lily's heart stuck in her throat as her dad came around the other side of the barn.

"Hi, Dad." She wished she didn't sound like she had been running, but she was scared he didn't want to be with Josie.

"I'd like you to help me clean up."

"Alyssa?"

Josie came around the other side of the barn. Lily looked from Josie to her dad and back again, but they weren't looking at each other.

Nuts. This wasn't working out at all.

"Okay, Daddy." Lily looked at her friend. "C'mon, Alyssa, you can help me."

"That's fine," her dad said. "I think Ms. Josie wants to go."

Lily gave her friend a quick look over her shoulder. Looked like her prayer didn't work after all. She waggled her fingers at Alyssa, then followed her dad back to the fire while Alyssa and Josie went in the opposite direction.

Silas fitted another nail into the board and slammed it home. The trouble light, hanging from the center beam of the ceiling of the cabin, swung from the force of his blows. He wished he had his Estwing, but he'd stupidly left that and his tool belt at the Old Town Hall, thinking he would be back on Monday.

One day he'd have to go back and pick up his things. He'd just have to choose his time. For now the hammer he found worked just fine.

He should be in the house with his little girl, but he couldn't face her. For the past two days she'd been peppering him with questions he didn't feel like answering.

Why wasn't he working on the Old Town Hall anymore? Why did he wait in his truck when he picked her up from the church? When was Ms. Josie coming again? Wasn't it fun to have her and Lily here? Was he going to see her again?

He wasn't. He'd made a colossal mistake kissing Josie the other day and if it weren't for the fact that it was convenient to keep Lily in the after-school program, he'd cancel that, as well.

Silas lowered his hammer, his eyes staring at the bent-over nail in front of him, but his mind was drifting back to that fateful evening three days ago.

Too easily he remembered the feel of Josie's lips on his, how she fitted so well in his arms.

She made his heart beat faster, she made his breath come quicker. She made him feel again. She made him feel that maybe he could love again.

These were the feelings he was outrunning. Getting out

of his system by working day and night on these cabins. Josie was becoming important to him. Was becoming someone he cared for.

The thought terrified him.

Only a few weeks ago he'd tested the extent of the pain he'd been hiding. Thanks to Josie he allowed it to come out. Up until then he had managed to keep the hurt of losing Kelly buried.

Now that he'd allowed it to come out, he knew even more than before how dangerous it was to put your heart into the hands of another human being and how much it could hurt.

He'd been wrong to listen to Josie. Wrong to let himself experience that pain. Losing Kelly had ripped his heart in two and the repairing of that had been a jagged, messy process. But he felt as if he had put it behind him.

Now, his feelings for Josie were changing each time he saw her. Changing and getting stronger.

Part of him felt as if he was betraying his wife's memory by getting involved with Josie.

But a bigger part of him wondered if he dared put himself in that vulnerable position of loving again. If he dared put himself into the position of potentially having his heart broken.

He knew that Josie had plans. That she wanted to move on. He didn't know where he fit in her life or if he dared assume anything.

Better to keep his heart whole and free because the pain of loving was too great. A picture of Josie slipped into his mind and he grabbed a hammer and tried to chase it away.

"Thanks again for lunch," Klaas said, setting the empty cup on the makeshift table.

Josie knew her smile was forced, but under the circumstances it was the best she had to offer.

It had been three days since the wiener roast. Three days since Silas had rocked her world with his kiss.

And in those three days he hadn't come once to work on the Old Town Hall. Nor had he called. When he came to the after-school program to pick up Lily he stayed in his truck.

Josie tidied up the leftovers from lunch and glanced at the clock. In twenty minutes she had to pick up her grandmother and bring her to her doctor's appointment. Then she had to rush back to be at the church before the children arrived.

The men had a job they wanted to finish before they had lunch, so Josie was left waiting, trying not to let her schedule take over her life.

Too busy, she thought. *Too many things on the go.*

What are you trying to prove?

Silas's words resonated through her mind and she brushed them aside as quickly as they were formulated. She wasn't trying to prove anything. She just liked to be involved. To help.

She put the remainder of the squares she had made for a snack on a disposable plate and wrapped them up with plastic wrap so the men would have something for later.

One quick glance around the kitchen showed her she was done. She put the garbage in a bag, then headed toward the door. She reached out for the handle just as the door opened toward her. Startled, she jumped back.

And Silas stepped through the door.

He looked up just as she caught her balance but not her equilibrium.

The mere sight of his tall figure, square-jawed features and level brows sent her heart into overdrive.

"What are you doing here?" she asked, putting a note of challenge into her voice.

Silas's gaze barely flicked over her, moving past to a pile of tools in the corner of the kitchen.

"Come to get my tool belt." He jerked his chin toward the corner.

"We haven't seen you around here much," Josie said as he strode past her, his booted feet echoing on the wooden floor.

"Been too busy," he muttered, bending over to pick up his tools.

"Working on your cabins?"

"That and other things." He straightened, his hands clutching his belt, his eyes everywhere but looking at her.

"Will you be coming again?"

She wished she could stop. Wished she didn't care that he wasn't coming. That he wasn't talking to her. That he hadn't called.

Sure, it was just a kiss, but she wasn't naive enough to think that a kiss between two people with their history had much innocence attached to it.

And his kiss had thrown her own world topsy-turvy. She foolishly thought it had moved him as much as it had moved her.

But there he stood, his weight on one hip, his tool belt swinging from his other hand, looking completely in control of his life and his emotions.

"I think my work is done here," he said, his gruff voice creating an unwelcome lilt to her heart.

But following that, came the anger.

How like a man to think he could kiss her, woo her, then simply drop out of her life without one word of explanation.

"I don't think it is," Josie said, deliberately keeping her eyes on his. "I don't think you're done at all."

Silas sighed. "I told you I was sorry. It was a mistake."

Why did it hurt the second time even more than the first?

"How can you say that? You knew full well what you were doing. You're not an impulsive person." Josie took a step forward, as if to underline her position.

Silas shoved his hand through his hair. "Look, this isn't getting us anywhere." But as he glanced at her, she caught a glimmer of the emotions she caught in his eyes just before he kissed her the first time.

"Why aren't you coming anymore, Silas? Is it because you're afraid of running into me?"

Silas swung his tool belt back and forth, back and forth, as if he was thinking. He avoided her gaze as he shook his head.

"No."

His single word gave her a glimmer of hope. "Then why?"

Back and forth. Back and forth.

"It's because...because of Kelly," Silas said, his eyes downcast, his mouth set in a grim line. "Working here has brought back too many memories of her."

Josie felt as if he had hit her with the hammer swinging from his tool belt.

"I thought you had worked through the grief? I thought you said you were ready to move on."

"Guess I wasn't." He glanced up at her, then away. "Working here makes me realize... Makes me remember how much it can hurt."

Her heart flopped over once, then began pounding in earnest, pushing against her ribs.

"Don't you think you need to remember the stories, even if they hurt?" Josie asked.

Part of her wanted to let go. To let Silas molder in his own grief.

But she had hoped that exorcising the memories meant working through them. She had hoped this would allow him to move on.

"Hiding away from your memories, pushing them down will only make them stronger and twist them into something evil and wrong." Josie gave her words a chance to settle. "You can face the memories with God's help. He is a father who loves us and His love is eternal. Before Kelly and you and I were even here, God's love was and is here."

Silas dropped his tool belt with a thump and took a step toward her. "Why do you care so much? Why does what I have to deal with matter to you?"

Josie swallowed at the emotions he rained down on her.

"What do you know about loss?" His words pounded at her. "What do you know about how much reliving the memories can make you afraid?"

Josie's frustration built, pushing at her defenses. Finally she could hold back no longer. "How dare you say that? You don't have a corner on grief or pain. I lost a dearly beloved sister and a brother-in-law. I lost both my parents when I was young. I live with a bitter, selfish woman whom I can't leave now because she needs me." The words and pain spilled out of her and she couldn't stop their onrushing flow. "Don't tell me I don't know about grief and grieving. Or about living with the consequences of loving someone. Every day I'm trying to please a woman who can't be pleased. A woman who is sucking the life out of me and my niece. A woman who won't let me forget who I once was. A woman I wanted to get away from but can't because this lousy tornado spun my life completely around and took away my last bit of independence from her." Josie's throat thickened on the last words and she stopped, pressing her hand against her lips as if trying to hold back anything else that might spill out. She had never told anyone how she felt about her grandmother and the influence she had on her life. She had been reminded enough times how unselfish her grandmother had been, taking her and her sister in.

And how unlike that Josie was.

"So leaving is the only way you can think of getting away from her?"

"I told you what I've had to live with."

Silas shook his head. "You accuse me of ignoring the past. I think you've spent too much time there. I think you

eed to move on in your mind before you do anything else.
think if you move now, you're just running away again."

"I know what I am, Silas."

"Maybe I know what I am. Maybe I also know what I can
nd can't take. What I dare risk."

The silence between them lengthened, and Josie felt the
eight of their words.

Silas's steady gaze locked on hers. Then he spoke. "Are
ou still thinking of leaving?"

Josie returned him look for look, trying to keep up with
is sudden switch in the conversation, wondering if he had
ven heard what she said.

"Why do you care about my plans," she shot back. "They
bviously won't affect you one way or the other. You won't
ive me anything to go on."

"I can't."

Josie blew out a sigh of exasperation. "Can't, or won't?"

"I can't deal with the grief. Losing Kelly hurt so much. I
oved her."

"Grief is the price we pay for love," she said, her anger inter-
upting him. "But it's worth the cost. Yes, loving hurts, and I'm
ure the memories of your wife can hurt, and it might be simpler
o keep them buried. But I'd sooner cry and feel and grieve and
naybe live in the past too much. But at least I live my life and
don't shut myself off from other people and from God the way
ou have and the way you have from your little girl."

And the way you have from me, she wanted to add, but
idn't dare. She couldn't take the chance of letting him know
ow much she cared for him.

Letting him know how much he had come to mean to her.

"You don't understand." His expression softened and he
rushed his finger over her cheek, stroking away the tear she
adn't even known she had shed.

She wanted to pull away, but expectation hovered between
nem, full of promise.

"Why don't you let me try?"

He pulled in a long, slow breath as a smile trembled on his lips. "You scare me, you know."

"And you scare me." She took a step nearer, letting him know that she understood.

She knew what he was going to do. Her senses heightened, and she couldn't move away.

"Josie." Her name came out on an anguished whisper. Then he bent his head and kissed her again.

Josie's world tilted and spun, her anger melting away like frost before the sun. She caught him by the shoulder and kissed him back.

Kissing him, being held by him, felt good and right and true. Josie moved and laid her head in the hollow of his shoulder and closed her eyes. He held her close, his head bent over her.

Josie opened her eyes, her heart battling with her mind. She shouldn't have let him kiss her nor should she have kissed him back.

But it felt so right.

You're leaving. You have your plans.

But she didn't want to think about her plans. She wanted to cling to the hope that their kisses had created.

Did she dare rearrange her life around a possibility? Did she dare think things would change between her and her grandmother?

Her doubts and fears made her pull away and be the first, this time, to break the connection.

He looked at her, his expression puzzled.

"We shouldn't have done that," she said.

He blinked, as if coming back to earth, then he nodded. "You're right. I'm sorry. That wasn't fair to Kelly."

In spite of her own second thoughts, his words sent an arrow of pain through her heart. It was still all about Kelly. Self-pity and confusion loomed ahead of her, and Josie tried o beat the emotions away. She couldn't let herself enter that place. If she did, who would pull her out?

She was all alone now.

"I gotta go," he muttered.

Then he was striding away from her, each step he took keeping time to the pounding of her heart.

Josie found her way home, her heart and mind battling, either gaining ground.

"Is that you, Josie?" her grandmother called out as Josie stepped into the house. "You took your time, didn't you?"

Josie closed her eyes and leaned against the door, praying or patience. Her emotions had gone through turmoil. She ad opened her heart to the possibilities of Silas and her, but eality had shattered the fragile dream. Silas still loved his wife. His perfect and loving wife who had never done nything wrong. Who was nothing like Josie Cane.

Why had she allowed herself to fall into the dream? She'd ad her life mapped out, her plans made.

"The doctor called," Betty said as she rolled her chair into he kitchen. "Cancelled the appointment. So you don't have o cart me around. I know you don't want to, in spite of everything I've put up with from you."

Josie looked at her grandmother, and as her bitterness ame at her, she remembered Silas's words about letting her randmother bring up her past. She didn't have to put up with . And in spite of what had just happened between her and ilas, she felt the assurance of his belief that her grandmother had no right to judge her. That in Christ, she was a ew creature.

She felt strength and determination course through her as he walked to the telephone. She picked it up, dialed her iend's number in Ohio and turned to look at her grandmother.

"Hey, Anne, Josie here. You still got room in your apartent? Great."

Betty's face grew red, but Josie kept her focus on what she needed. What Alyssa needed. There was nothing for her here Except Nicki. But she couldn't stay simply for her friend's sake.

As she and Anne made plans, one part of her mind slipped over her friends here in High Plains. She thought of the good times she'd had the past few years and her determination wavered.

But when she thought of facing Silas, who couldn't forget his wife, she knew she couldn't stay. Not anymore.

Chapter Fourteen

Silas threw his pouch onto the porch floor, kicked off his boots and stormed into the kitchen.

What had he been thinking? What had he done?

Kissed Josie Cane again, that's what he'd done.

He dropped one hip against the counter as he dragged his hands over his face.

He thought staying away from her would have eased the ache in his gut whenever he thought of her. Would ease the awful emptiness that had taken over his life.

But what did he do mere minutes after seeing her again? After listening to a mini lecture about life and pain and grief?

He kissed her.

She didn't ask him to. Didn't invite it. After his little lecture about missing Kelly and the pain of loving, he made the first move down a path that could only cause him more pain.

Why not take a chance? Why not take a risk? She feels the same way about you.

Silas wished he could still the voice in his head. He had spent the past few days trying to still the optimistic thoughts.

Loving Kelly had brought him pain.

But it also brought you joy.

He wasn't putting himself through that again.

And what about the loneliness? The times you miss having someone around?

Silas slammed his hand on the countertop. "I can't face i again."

The sound of his voice echoed through the kitchen and fo a moment he felt utterly foolish. This was how bad thing were getting. He was talking to himself.

Even worse, he had lied to Josie. When he had held he in his arms he had felt as if love was a possibility in his life again. As if a future might contain light and hope and woman he could love.

Then fear had made him hide behind Kelly, and he had le Josie think he couldn't come to care for her because of Kelly Yes, he still loved his wife, but that was the past. Not the future

Silas pushed himself away from the counter and strode out of the kitchen. He took the stairs two at a time, pulled off the clean shirt he had put on just to go to town and tosse it into a corner.

He needed to get to work. To keep going. To keep at bay all thoughts of Josie. To silence the voices. To remind himsel that he'd had a wife and that he'd shared enough with Kelly Enough happiness and enough sorrow.

As he pulled open his dresser drawer his eyes fell on the picture Lily had given him for his birthday. The picture o Josie Cane laughing at the camera.

Her smile and the sparkle of mischief in her eyes slowed his hands as he pulled a shirt out of the drawer.

Forget it. Just keep going. Remember Kelly.

But he dropped the shirt and picked up the picture, looking at it more closely. And layered over his previously raging emotions came a vague sense of peace.

And a long-forgotten feeling that was a potent mixture o attraction, yearning and…love?

He pushed the emotion down. No. He couldn't.

Josie was quickly becoming too important to him and to is daughter. He felt as if each minute he spent with her put nother hook into his heart.

The tearing away would be more than he could bear.

Yet he traced her features, wondering. She hadn't denied hat she was leaving. And in spite of his brave words to her, e didn't blame her. As long as her grandmother had a hold ver her, Josie couldn't let go of the past.

His own feelings were a morass of confusion and grew eeper each time he saw her. If he didn't stop this, it would nly cause more hurt in the end.

But what end?

What lay ahead for him and his daughter? More lonely days?

His mind skipped over the times he and Lily had spent vith Josie and Alyssa. The last time had held a feeling of ompleteness. Of a family.

Silas dropped onto the bed, setting Josie's picture aside. Ie was at a crossroads in his life, unsure which way to turn. Ie wanted safety and he yearned for peace. But staying way from Josie had only increased the raging thoughts pinning through his head.

He wanted to be a faithful husband and he had been. But vas coming to care for Josie denying his love for his wife? Denying the memory he'd only lately begun to explore?

His eyes fell on the Bible lying beside his bed. It had once elonged to Kelly. He wondered what she would think of osie. Wondered if she would approve.

Was he being disloyal to his wife? Was he wrong to acnowledge his changing feelings for Josie?

His head tightened with questions and confusion. Vouldn't he be better off to keep to himself? To keep his eart whole and his life uncomplicated?

He'd been married. He'd been in love. Kelly had been a ood and faithful wife. Many men don't experience that even nce in their lifetime.

But if Josie didn't return his feelings all his question were just dust in the wind.

Silas reached across the bed and took the Bible off the en table. He thought of a passage he had read the other day whe he couldn't sleep. When his mind was tossed between hi changing feelings for Josie and his changing feelings for hi wife's memory.

He flipped open the Bible to the bookmark and bega reading.

"As a father has compassion on his children, so the Lor has compassion on those who fear Him; for He knows ho we are formed, He remembers that we are dust. As for mar his days are like grass, he flourishes like a flower of the fielc the wind blows over it and it is gone, and its place remem bers it no more."

A wave of sadness washed over him as he read thos words. Josie had accused him of stifling the pain of losin, Kelly so much that he was losing the memories. Losing th memories meant losing the stories for Lily. He didn't war Kelly to be merely a fleeting memory and yet he also knev there came a time when he would have to move on.

Would he want Josie beside him then?

He turned back to the passage. "But from everlasting t everlasting the Lord's love is with those who fear Him, an His righteousness with their children's children—with thos who keep His covenant and remember to obey His precepts.

He set the Bible aside and stared off into the middle dis tance, the words he had just read resonating through his minc

God's love was faithful, enduring and eternal. Like father's love for his children and as high as the Heaven above the earth. Kelly had reminded him of that with her las few breaths. Josie had reminded him just the other day.

Josie had also told him that the potential for grief was price worth paying.

Deep in his heart, he knew it to be true. But was he read; to open himself up to it?

* * *

"We are in trouble." Lily glanced over at Ms. Josie, then back at her friend. The two girls had scooted off into a corner of the classroom behind the bulletin board that Ms. Josie used to separate the class area from the play area to discuss the latest wrinkle in their plan. "My daddy was really quiet yesterday and when I asked him what was wrong, he said nothing. And he looked a bit mad."

Alyssa spun her hair around her finger and pulled her lower lip between her teeth. "Auntie Josie was kinda sad yesterday and I don't know why. And she told me that we're probably moving in a couple of weeks."

Lily pulled her knees up to her chest and held her one hand up. "We gave your aunt a picture of my dad and my dad has a picture of your aunt. We got them together for dinner." She ticked each of these off on her fingers. "Then we got them together for a wiener roast. And then we prayed." She looked with dismay at her hand with all the fingers up. "What else can we do?"

"I'm scared," Alyssa said, hugging her legs. "I don't want to move away to Ohio, but Auntie Josie's friend keeps calling her and saying how excited she is we're coming."

Lily puffed up her cheeks and released her breath. "I have one more idea, but I don't know if it will work."

"What's that?"

Lily leaned closer to her friend. "I took my dad's jacket to school today. I thought we could bring it to your house. Then you can phone my dad and tell him that he left his coat at the Old Town Hall and that it's at your place."

"Didn't he see the coat in your backpack?"

"Nope. I always make my own lunch and pack my own backpack."

"When do I phone him?"

"Tonight. At about six."

"Will he be there on time?"

"My dad is always on time," Lily said.

"Auntie Josie said we were going to be gone, but I'll try to make sure we're back on time." Alyssa gave her friend a feeble smile.

A shiver trickled down Lily's back. "Do you think this will work?"

"It has to," Alyssa said. Then she sat up, looking scared. "Should we have prayed about it? Do you think God is mad at us for bothering Him with this?"

"Didn't you tell me that we should tell God everything? Didn't you tell me that He loves us like a dad?"

Alyssa nodded.

"Well, then I think we should have prayed. Because this is important. I know my daddy was happy and that he was smiling the last few weeks. And he hasn't done that in a long time."

Lily heard the sound of footsteps and then Ms. Josie was standing over top of them.

"What are you two scheming back here?"

She said it like it was supposed to be a joke, but Ms. Josie wasn't smiling. Actually, Ms. Josie hadn't smiled much since her dad stopped working on the Old Town Hall.

"We're just talking," Alyssa said quickly. "Friend talk."

Ms. Josie squatted down. "That's good talk to have." Then she stroked Alyssa's hair and tucked a piece behind her ear.

Lily was suddenly jealous of her friend, and even more determined to bring her daddy and Ms. Josie together.

Ms. Josie turned to Lily and then, to Lily's surprise, she stroked her hair, too.

Her heart got big in her chest and she thought maybe she was going to be like a little sissy and start crying. But she wasn't going to cry.

And she knew she wasn't going to give up. She wanted Ms. Josie for a mother more than anything she had wanted since her mother died.

She gave Alyssa a secret look and carefully pointed to her backpack. Alyssa nodded. Hopefully she knew exactly what Lily meant.

"Are you sure it's my jacket?" Silas planted one hand on his hip as he held the handset of the phone with the other, wondering why Alyssa was the one to make the call and not Josie. "I don't remember taking it along."

"My aunt said it was yours." Alyssa Cane sounded a bit breathless, like she'd been running. "She found it just a couple of days ago."

Silas remembered missing his jacket a couple of days ago. Maybe he left it at the Old Town Hall the last time he'd gone there, a week ago.

When he'd kissed Josie again.

He'd gone over that kiss so many times, veering from thinking he shouldn't have done it to the reality of how right it felt. He was so sure Josie returned his feelings.

But he knew he shouldn't expect that she would call him or try to contact him. In the course of trying to protect himself, he'd sent out a stream of mixed messages the last time he'd seen her. Kissing her. Then making her think that he still harbored feelings for his wife.

"Could you come tonight?" Alyssa was asking. "At seven o'clock?"

Silas frowned, the faint niggle of a premonition sifting through the conversation. However, the thought of seeing Josie again, or explaining himself to her, pushed aside any second thought he might have.

"My aunt and I will be gone," Alyssa said. "In case that's a problem. But I'll leave it with Gramma."

Diasappointment slithered through him. Guess he wouldn't have a chance to talk to her. "Sure, I'll be there."

"At seven o'clock," Alyssa reminded him.

"On the dot." Silas said a puzzled goodbye then ended the phone call just as Lily came into the kitchen.

"What was that about?" she asked in a very adult voice as she dropped onto a kitchen chair.

"My jacket is at Ms. Cane's place. I'm picking it up." He leveled a piercing look at his daughter, wondering if she and Alyssa were up to something, but she gave him a careful smile and nodded. "Can I stay home or do you want me to come with you?"

"I'm not comfortable with leaving you here by yourself."

"I'm a big girl, Daddy."

She sounded so confident, so sure of herself, he felt a pang of yearning. She was growing up. But she wasn't that big yet. Not big enough to be left here, all alone. He felt again the weight of responsibility. Then he smiled and held his hand out to her. "We'll go together," he said, his voice firm.

The drive to town was quiet. Lily stared out the window, humming to herself.

Silas kept his eyes on the darkening road as the sun hovered at the horizon. In a month the sun would be gone this time of the evening.

And so the seasons slip by, he thought with a touch of melancholy.

It had now been more than two years since Kelly had died. Two years since he wondered how he was going to carry on. But he had. Day by day, week by week. His work on the ranch and taking care of Lily had kept him occupied and slowly he had found a new rhythm.

Now, thanks to Josie, he had found a new way to handle the grief of his wife's death. And, thanks to Josie, he had found a new purpose to his life.

He clutched the steering wheel, willing the emotions away. He was doing the right thing, keeping his heart whole and safe. Word about town was that Josie was leaving. The thought sent a wave of panic through him, followed by the firm resolve that he had done the right thing in staying away from her. Lily needed a father who was here for her, not yearning after a woman who was leaving.

But what if he told her how he felt? Would that change anything?

Did he dare?

Silas felt the wavering of indecision and then, as he imagined his life without Josie in it, he knew he had to at least try. He pulled up to the cabin ten minutes early. His heart thudded in his chest when he saw Josie's car. Here was his chance.

"Just wait in the truck, honey," he said to Lily. "I'll be right back." He pulled open the door and hoped he could face Josie if she was there.

As he walked up the steps he saw someone walking past the window. He peered through the window of the door and frowned.

Josie's grandmother? Walking around the kitchen?

He knocked on the door to warn her and then opened it.

Betty Carter whirled around, a knife in one hand, a jar of peanut butter in the other hand and a guilty look on her face.

"What are you doing here?" she snapped.

"I've come for my coat," Silas said, glancing from her to the wheelchair situated just inside the doorway between the kitchen and the living room. He frowned. "I thought you couldn't walk?"

Betty looked quickly away, clutching the edge of the counter. "Sometimes I can." She swayed and Silas was just about to catch her when he caught her glancing at him over her shoulder, as if to make sure he had seen.

He stopped. "You can walk just fine, can't you?"

Betty lowered her knife and turned to face him. "What business is that of yours?"

Silas held her gaze. "Why are you pretending? Do you know how much Josie worries about you?"

Betty let go an unladylike snort. "That girl doesn't care

about me at all. Never did. She always went her own way. Did her own thing. Always was selfish."

A surprising anger washed over him. "How can you say that about her?" he retorted. "Josie genuinely cares about you and has helped more people in this town than you could ever know about." Silas's anger grew as he thought of the doctor's appointments Josie had arranged, the concern she had repeatedly expressed over her grandmother's failure to walk. "And this is how you repay her? By pretending to be sicker than you really are? By pretending you can't walk?"

Betty looked away, her mouth pressed in mutinous lines. "You don't know what I've had to put up with. That girl has been trouble from the day she was born. And after all I did for her, she's moving away." Betty gave him a narrowed look. "You be careful around her. That girl is trouble. She's nothing like your dead wife."

Through his growing anger Silas heard one word.

Silas's hands clenched at his side as he fought down his temper. How could Betty have deceived Josie? How did she dare hide behind her injury just to protect her feelings? How weak. How selfish.

But as he glared at Betty, the angry words echoed in his mind. Then shame crept in behind his own anger.

Hadn't he just done the same thing to Josie?

Hadn't he just hidden behind his grieving for Kelly to keep himself from Josie? From the potential of pain?

He was no better than Josie's grandmother.

"Why are you so hard on her?" he asked, struggling to still his anger and his shame at his own deception of a person who deserved so much more. "Josie has been a good granddaughter to you. Yes, she has made mistakes in the past, but who hasn't—"

Betty waggled her finger at Silas, as if admonishing him. "You don't know the half of what she's done. I'll bet she's never told you—"

"I don't care what she's done." The words fairly burst out of him before he could stop them. And he didn't care that he had interrupted her. He had something to say that he couldn't seem to hold back anymore. "God has forgiven her even if she doesn't seem to realize that. And as for what she used to be, I only care what she is right now—one of the best people I know. She is unselfish to a fault. She is more giving than anyone I've ever met. She is kinder and gentler than even Kelly ever was."

"She was," Betty protested.

"Josie is more than her equal. In fact, I think Josie is even kinder and more generous."

"But I thought you loved your wife? That you couldn't get over her death." Betty seemed shocked that he spoke that way about Kelly.

"I loved Kelly dearly. And hopefully, with God's help, I've dealt with the grief I felt over her death. But I also know the time has come to move on. To know that I love Josie. To know that I love her more than I thought I could ever love anyone again." He stopped as the words he just spoke resonated between them, filling the cabin.

"I love her," he said again, his words coming out in an astonished whisper.

He dragged one hand over his face as he grabbed the back of a nearby chair with another to steady himself. He knew it to be true and right. He loved Josie Cane.

Then he caught Betty's astonished glance, but she wasn't looking at him.

She was looking over his shoulder.

With a sinking feeling of inevitability, Silas turned.

Behind him, framed in the doorway, the light from the porch behind her making a nimbus of gold around her face, stood Josie.

Chapter Fifteen

Josie clung to the doorway as a sailor would the mast of a storm-tossed ship. Her eyes held Silas's steady gaze and as he walked toward her, the ground beneath her tilted and turned.

What had he said?

Did he mean it?

He came to a halt in front of her, his hands hanging at his sides as if unsure of what to do with them.

"Did you say—" Josie cleared her throat and tried again. "Did you say that you love me?"

She swallowed down the emotions threatening to swamp her. In her peripheral vision she saw her grandmother move to a kitchen chair. She heard Alyssa running out of the house behind her.

All these things she pushed aside as unimportant.

Right now she needed to keep her head clear and her focus on Silas.

His gaze was on her, his brown eyes holding hers intently.

"I love you, Josie Cane." His simple declaration knocked the ground out from under her and she would have fallen, but Silas caught her. Pulled her into the haven of his arms.

He cradled her head against his shoulder with one hand,

rapped his other arm completely around her, clutching her aist. "I'm so sorry. I was so wrong. What I said about Kelly asn't true, but I was afraid to love you. Afraid to let you to my life, but I do love you. I do."

Josie let his words wash over her, let his arms hold her . The beginnings of a sob caught in her throat but she ught it down. Gently she eased her head back. She needed see his beloved face.

She cupped her hands around his cheeks, stroking their ugh texture with her thumbs as she made her simple declara- n.

"I love you."

Silas looked down at her, his expression serious. "I was wrong," he murmured. "I was hiding behind my feelings r Kelly. I'm sorry."

"I won't hurt you" was all she could say. "I'll never hurt u."

"But you already have." Silas let a smile slip over his lips. e pressed her hand against his chest. "Right now this hurts. ut it hurts good. I'd be lying if I said I wasn't scared ymore. That I trust God will help me through anything that ight happen to you, or Lily or Alyssa. But you were right. etter to live with the potential of pain than to live with the rety of loneliness." He laid his forehead against hers and osed his eyes. "I don't want you to go. I don't want you to ave High Plains."

Josie thought of her plans. They had been so important to r at one time. But now, here in Silas's arms, they lost their gency.

"I know you feel you have to leave," he continued, pulling vay to look at her. "To protect Alyssa. And to protect urself." Silas glanced over his shoulder at Betty, who still t watching the two of them, then he turned his loving gaze ck on her. "But I want you to know that I'm here for you. believe in you and know who you are. You are such an amazing person I can't let you out of my life. I want to protect you from every harsh word, every false rumor. But if you still feel you need to leave..." He let the sentence trail off, as if he wasn't sure what she would do, as if he was giving her permission to make up her own mind.

Josie lost herself in his earnest gaze as his hands clung to her arms, as his words washed over her, comforting and strengthening.

"I don't think I'm going anywhere," she whispered. She felt as if she didn't need to run. To hide. She wasn't alone anymore.

She had Silas.

"I don't want to go. Not anymore," she said, conviction ringing in her voice. What could she possibly find anywhere else better than what she had right here, right now?

He smiled. "I love you so much."

"I love you, too" was all Josie could say.

She pulled his head down to hers and she sealed her promise with a warm, gentle, kiss.

Then she drew away and looked at her grandmother watching them. With Silas's arm around her to give her strength, Josie faced her grandmother.

"Why did you do it? Why did you pretend you couldn't walk?"

"I was going to tell you," Betty said, avoiding the question.

"When?" Silas asked.

Betty's gaze shot to his, then down again. "When I knew she wasn't going to leave."

Josie frowned, then went to her grandmother's side and knelt so she could look up at her. "What do you mean?"

Betty sighed, her fingers twisted around each other. "I thought you would stay if you thought I couldn't walk."

"But surely you couldn't keep this up forever."

Betty nodded. "I know. But I thought as long as I could

ou would stay here. And then you started making plans and didn't know what to do anymore."

Josie wanted to be angry with Betty, but her grandmother's deception had stalled Josie's plans long enough for er and Silas to find each other. And for that, she could orgive her grandmother's deception many, many times over.

Josie covered Silas's hand with hers and glanced over her houlder at him.

Silas caught her smile and dropped another kiss on her orehead. "We should go get the girls."

Josie's smile grew. "I'm sure they'll be pleased."

"And they should be." Silas held her gaze and stroked her ingers with his. "And so am I."

She turned just in time to see Lily and Alyssa standing in the loorway holding hands, watching them with avid expressions.

"I guess we don't need to tell them anything," Josie said. I think they know what's going on here."

Lily glanced at Alyssa, raised her hand and her friend igh-fived her. "It worked," Alyssa said with a grin. "Our act worked."

Josie didn't ask. She didn't want to know.

"Your grandmother has been able to walk the whole ime?" Nicki closed the folder on her desk and slipped it into he filing cabinet.

"Not the whole time, but for a while. She didn't want me o leave High Plains." Josie leaned her hip against Nicki's esk, glancing around the schoolroom. Colorful leaves anced along the top of the blackboard and a few pictures of umpkins decorated the bulletin board. Pretty soon it would e Thanksgiving. And how much didn't Josie have to be hankful for this year.

"Some strange kind of love she has for you," Nicki said.

"At least I know she cares."

"And you know Silas cares."

Josie caught a pensive tone in her friend's voice and shot her a puzzled look. "What's the matter, Nicki?"

But Nicki waved one slender hand, as if brushing the question aside.

"Nicki. Tell me."

"It's nothing."

Josie tried to catch her friend's gaze. "Are you still worried about Kasey?"

"That...and other things."

"Other things being Clay?"

"No. Of course not Clay. He's long gone." Nicki's voice held a note of scorn. "He hasn't even bothered to come back to town to check on his family after this devastating tornado. People who care should do that, right?" Nicki's eyes snapped with surprising anger.

But Josie heard a subtext to her friend's words. Clay not only hadn't bothered to find out about his family, Clay hadn't bothered to find out about *her.* Josie put a comforting hand on her shoulder. "If he doesn't care, you're better off without him."

"So people seem to think." Nicki pressed her lips together, as if holding back her next comment. Then she forced a smile and looked at her friend. "So. Silas Marstow and Josie Cane. Tell me all the details."

Josie wanted to tell her so much, but she felt a nudge of guilt at her own happiness.

"All the details," Nicki emphasized, her smile more genuine this time. "Because thanks to the man, I'm guessing you're sticking around."

"Yes. For now." Nothing had been settled. Nothing had been said, but Josie was happy enough to be courted for now. "It's early days. Really early days, but he's been great. He's at my grandmother's house right now putting the pressure on the contractor to get the work done soon and he's been helping me with paperwork for the insurance company for my house. It won't be done for Christmas, but it will be soon."

Nicki leveled her friend a wry look. "House supervision? Paperwork for insurance companies? How romantic."

"Well, what else can I say?"

"Silas Marstow? Tall, broodingly good-looking? I'm sure you could say a lot. You have to tell me all the details. How did you find out that he cared? What did he say? How did he say it?" Nicki held her hand up. "More important, is he a good kisser?"

Josie frowned at her friend and was about to reprimand her when a discreet knock at the door drew their attention.

Josie's cheeks turned bright red when she saw who was there.

Tall, broodingly handsome Silas Marstow. He was wearing a denim jacket, clean blue jeans and a smile.

"I was wondering if I could borrow Josie for a while?"

Nicki winked at her friend. "Mr. Marstow, she's all yours."

"Do you have some time, Josie?" Silas asked. "I need to talk to you outside."

"Sure. Let me get my jacket." Josie ignored Nicki's grin and got her coat from the table she had thrown it on. As she went to meet Silas, her heart rose in expectation.

Just seeing him made her feel all giddy and young again. Love did that to a person, she thought, her smile growing as her eyes met his.

"I just got back from your grandmother's house," Silas said as she joined him. "Things are coming along really well."

"I'm glad." Josie released her breath on a sigh of thankfulness. For the past week it was as if one weight after another had been lifted off her shoulders.

"Any word on my house?" Josie asked as they stepped out the door.

Silas scratched his forehead with his finger as he chewed

his lower lip. "Not promising much. Now that the insurance company okayed the paperwork, it will take time to find someone who can get everything done before winter comes. Most of the good guys are swamped."

"So unless I want to move in with my grandmother, I'll be living at the Waters cottage until it's finished." The cottage was cozy, but she longed to be back in her own house where there was space for her and Alyssa. And, whenever they came over for dinner, space for Silas and Lily, as well. She gave him a careful smile. "Guess you never fully realized what you would be taking on when you started dating me?"

Silas gave her a crooked smile as he tucked a wayward strand of hair behind her ear. He tucked her arm in his and walked toward the truck. "I knew from the start exactly what I was getting."

"So what did you need to talk to me about?"

"We need to check something at the Old Town Hall." Silas turned to her, the early-afternoon light casting his face into intriguing shadows.

Josie held his gaze, content for the moment to simply look at him. How much had changed from that moment, a few months ago, when his gaze had been full of anger, his mouth set in harsh lines.

Now his features looked more relaxed. Content. As if that pent-up anger had been eased from his life. And his eyes held a promise of future happiness.

"You sound very solemn," Josie teased, curious what this was about.

"I'm a serious guy," he said, and turned and walked toward the Old Town Hall.

Now she was really intrigued. And a bit concerned. Was he having second thoughts?

Josie pushed away the question. If anything, in the past few weeks she had discovered that Silas wasn't someone to trifle with people. Or their emotions. He did what he said he would do.

She followed him as he skirted the main building, walking to the back, overlooking the river.

The sun caught the tips of the waves as the water slipped past, throwing diamonds of light into the autumn air. Calm pervaded the air and Josie relaxed.

Silas came to a stop close to the edge of the river and turned as Josie joined him. He had his hands in the pockets of his denim jacket, and his eyes on the Old Town Hall behind them.

"Do you think it will get done on time for Founders' Day?" Josie asked, feeling a need to lighten the suddenly serious atmosphere.

"I'm sure it will," he said, turning his gaze back on her. "But if not, then I'm hoping it's done by another date."

Josie frowned. "Which one?"

Silas pulled a tiny velvet box out of his pocket and opened it. And the flashing of the sun on the water suddenly had competition.

Josie stared at the single diamond on the golden band and her heart expanded in her chest.

"Josie Cane, will you marry me?" Silas asked, reaching for her hand.

Josie grasped it, needing the solidity of his hand to hold her anchored to earth. She stared at the shining diamond, then lifted eyes glimmering with tears to Silas.

She couldn't say anything, the heavy pounding of her heart and the thickening of her throat robbing her of speech. All she could do was nod.

He slipped the ring on her finger. Then she was in his arms, being held close to his chest, his arms around her.

"I love you, Josie," he murmured in her ear. "And I want to spend the rest of my life letting you know that."

Josie pressed her damp cheek to his chest, then drew back. "I love you, Silas Marstow. And I'm praying that God will give us a long and happy life together."

They sealed their promise with a kiss.

And when they finally pulled away, Silas held her hand, letting the sun refract through the diamond. "I thought we could pick up the girls and go celebrate tonight."

"But I have to work."

Silas shook his head. "No. I've got that covered."

"Wow, you think of everything."

"I like to think I do." His hand cupped her face. "And I like to think that you won't have to worry about living in your house. I'd like to think that you won't need the house at all. If you're willing to live in the country, that is."

Josie's heart grew even larger. Living out in the country. Space for her, Silas, Lily and Alyssa.

"Sounds like a dream come true."

"I think it would be the best place to raise our new family. After all," he said with a wink, "we are going to need the space."

Silas dropped a kiss on her mouth, then drew her back to the truck. "I think I heard the bell for the end of school. Let's go get the girls and give them the news. Let them know how their little matchmaking pact turned out in the end."

"Let's just hope it doesn't go to their heads," Josie said, returning his smile.

"It will give them a good story to tell their future brothers and sisters."

"Amongst many other stories, I hope," Josie said.

"Many other stories," Silas agreed. "Some happy and some sad, I'm sure. But with God's help, all of them will have a thread of His grace woven through them."

"Amen to that," Josie whispered. They shared another kiss, then turned and stepped into the future.

* * * * *

Dear Reader,

I have never experienced a tornado, but I have experienced loss. I've also seen, up close, the effect that losing a home can have on a family and the effect that losing a loved one can have. The fictional people in High Plains have experienced both, and in my story I tried to show how Josie and Silas have dealt with their own particular losses—the loss of a home, the loss of a loved one and the loss of a reputation. I hope I've also shown that the God who wrapped himself in human form understands our sorrow and helps us carry it. I hope and pray that those of you who have experienced loss and grief in its many forms will turn to Him and trust that He will give you the rest He promises in the Bible.

P.S. I love to hear from my readers. Please write to me at caarsen@xplornet.com or check out my Web site at www.carolyneaarsen.com.

Carolyne Aarsen

QUESTIONS FOR DISCUSSION

1. Why do you think Josie felt the way she did about herself?

2. How would you have dealt with Josie's grandmother?

3. If you had lost someone you loved, as Silas did, how would you react?

4. Have you ever felt bitter about the events in your life? How did you deal with that?

5. The people of High Plains lost so much in so many ways. How do you think you would feel in their position?

6. Have you ever blamed God for your sorrows, as Silas did? How do you think God feels about that?

7. What was your reaction to how Silas dealt with his wife's death?

8. What would your reaction be to having two young girls meddling in your life?

9. One of the themes of this book is how we deal with the stories of the past and how we let them influence us. What was Silas's way of dealing with his past?

10. How did Josie deal with her past?

11. Not all single parents find their "happy ever after," as Silas and Josie did. What are some challenges for single parents today?

12. How could those of us who have a stable life help them?

13. Have you ever faced a life-changing challenge like the residents of High Plains? How did you deal with the situation?

14. What lessons do you think the people of High Plains should learn from the tornado?

15. If people are fortunate enough not to face disasters in life, how could they help those who do?

Turn the page for a preview of the next exciting
AFTER THE STORM *book*
A FAMILY FOR THANKSGIVING by Patricia Davids,
available in November from Love Inspired.

One second Nicki was walking down the sidewalk across from the construction site at Old Town Hall, and the next second her world tipped sideways.

Stumbling to a halt, she blinked and looked again. The mirage didn't vanish. The heavy thud of her heart stole her breath, leaving her numb with shock.

Clay Logan stood not fifty feet away, his hands shoved in the pockets of a brown sheepskin-lined jacket as he hunched against the cutting wind. It was only the second day of November, but the deep chill in the air was a reminder that winter wasn't far away.

What was Clay doing here? How long had he been back in town? How long was he staying?

He hadn't seen her. She was thankful for that small favor as she struggled to regain her composure. He was surveying a bare patch of earth ringed with old concrete footings. It was all that remained of the large gazebo that had once stood in the middle of the town's park.

Was he as saddened by its loss as she had been?

So much of the tornado-ravaged town was in the process of being rebuilt—homes, businesses, the historic Old Town Hall. Fixing the gazebo wasn't even on the list of things the overwhelmed city council had planned.

Besides, another gazebo would never be the same.

As if aware that someone was watching him, Clay turned to look in her direction. His shoulders stiffened. For a long instant they stared at each other without moving. Then, he touched the brim of his black cowboy hat to acknowledge her.

She wished she were closer, wished she could see the expression in his eyes.

Was the love still there?

Of course it wasn't. What a foolish thing to wonder. They'd been starry-eyed teenagers the last time they'd seen each other.

Don't just stand here. Walk away. Pretend it doesn't matter that he's back, she told herself.

She wouldn't let it matter. She'd wasted enough years of her life hoping for his return. Forcing herself to take a step, she flinched when she realized he was already moving toward her, closing the distance.

Turning around and running in the opposite direction suddenly seemed like a good idea. But running away was Clay's specialty, not hers.

The thought stiffened her spine. She shifted her large green-and-orange-striped tote to her other shoulder and waited. As he approached, she saw that the years had changed his good looks from boyish charm into chiseled masculinity.

Dark stubble covered his square chin and the planes of his cheeks. Crow's-feet at the corners of his deep blue eyes added character to his face, but the soft grin that pulled at one corner of his mouth was still the same one she remembered.

A swirl of butterflies filled her midsection. The sight of
that slow smile aimed in her direction used to melt her heart
like butter in a hot pan.

Stop. What am I doing?

Nicki gathered her scattered wits. Roguish grin or not, she
wasn't about to fall back into some bygone, teenage hero-
worship mode. She had far too much sense for that.

Time to start acting like it.

"As I live and breathe, if it isn't Clay Logan. I almost
didn't recognize you. What's it been, five years?" She was
proud that her tone carried just the right touch of indiffer-
ence. If only he didn't notice the white-knuckled grip she had
on the strap of her bag.

His smile disappeared. "It's been seven years, Nicki."

"That long?" She tsked as she shook her head. "Time
sure flies, doesn't it?"

She swept one hand toward the park, indicating the broken
trees and rubble piles that hadn't yet been removed. "As you
can see, things have changed a lot since you were here."

"I guess they have," he replied, a sad quality in his voice.
His gaze never left her.

Tipping her head to one side, she narrowed her eyes. "You
didn't really expect things would be the same as when you
left, did you?"

He pulled off his hat and ran his fingers through his dark
hair. "No, but I wasn't prepared for exactly how different
things would be."

At that moment, he looked lost and uncertain. Sympathy
eroded her ire. She'd had four months to become accus-
tomed to the scarred face of High Plains. He must be seeing
it for the first time. It had to be painful.

She said, "The tornado really made a mess of things. The
downtown area was hit pretty hard. The General Store is
gone, as are most of the homes south of Garrison Street
between First and Second."

Still holding his hat, he used it to point toward the line o
broken trees in the park that ran between the High Plain
River and the town's Main Street. "It's hard to believe onl
one person was killed."

"Yes, God was with us. The carriage house beside th
church and the Old Town Hall both took direct hits. Volun
teers from the community are rebuilding the hall, as you ca
see. The hope is that it'll be done in time to hold th
Founders' Day celebration on Christmas Day."

"Looks like they're making good progress."

"With the outside, yes, but the inside is still bare studs."

"What about you? Did you lose much?"

Waving a hand to dismiss her minor losses, she said, "A
broken window. That was all." And the photo of the two o
them that she'd tossed in the trash that night.

Hitching her bag higher, she flashed a bright smile. "
need to get going. It was good seeing you again, Clay."

Stepping around him, she was surprised when he reache
out and took hold of her elbow. "Nicki, I'm sorry."

*Don't do this, Clay. Not after all this time. I waited s
long for you.*

Keeping the smile on her face cost her dearly. Her chee
muscles ached with the effort. "What are you sorry about?

He studied her with a puzzled frown. "For taking off lik
that."

Was he really expecting her to just forgive him? To sa
the last seven years didn't matter? She had some pride. Ther
was no way she'd let him see how much he'd hurt her.

"It's water under the bridge, Clay. We were just kids.
wasn't like we were soul mates or something."

He didn't reply, but he released her. His hand dropped
his side. "I'm glad you didn't hold it against me."

Her mind screamed at her to leave before he saw throug
the veil she'd pulled over her turbulent emotions, but sh

couldn't stop drinking in the sight of him. The urge to fling
herself into his arms and hug him was overwhelming. Why
did he still have such an effect on her?

* * * * *

Look for A FAMILY FOR THANKSGIVING
by Patricia Davids
to read more about Clay and Nicki's reunion.
Available in November from Love Inspired.

Love Inspired®

HEARTWARMING INSPIRATIONAL ROMANCE

Get more of the heartwarming
inspirational romance stories that
you love and cherish, beginning
in July with SIX NEW titles,
available every month from
the Love Inspired® line.

Also look for our other
Love Inspired® genres, including:

Love Inspired® Suspense:
Enjoy four contemporary tales of intrigue
and romance every month.

Love Inspired® Historical:
Travel to a different time with two powerful
and engaging stories of romance, adventure
and faith every month.

Love Inspired

Tacy Jones had come to
Mule Hollow to train
wild horses—but
Brent Stockwell doesn't
think *ladies* belong in
the pen. So Tacy will just
have to change his mind!
But when she learns his
reason, she's determined
to show the handsome
cowboy that taking a
chance on your dream is
what life is all about.

Look for

His Cowgirl Bride
by
Debra Clopton

*Available November
wherever books are sold.*

www.SteepleHill.com

Steeple
Hill®
LI87563

REQUEST YOUR FREE BOOKS!

2 FREE INSPIRATIONAL NOVELS
PLUS 2
FREE
MYSTERY GIFTS

Love Inspired

YES! Please send me 2 FREE Love Inspired® novels and my 2 FREE mystery gifts (gifts are worth about $10). After receiving them, if I don't wish to receive any more books, I can return the shipping statement marked "cancel". If I don't cancel, I will receive 4 brand-new novels every month and be billed just $4.24 per book in the U.S. or $4.74 per book in Canada. That's a savings of over 20% off the cover price. It's quite a bargain! Shipping and handling is just 50¢ per book.* I understand that accepting the 2 free books and gifts places me under no obligation to buy anything. I can always return a shipment and cancel at any time. Even if I never buy another book, the two free books and gifts are mine to keep forever.

113 IDN EYK2   313 IDN EYLE

Name	(PLEASE PRINT)	
Address		Apt. #
City	State/Prov.	Zip/Postal Code
Signature (if under 18, a parent or guardian must sign)		

Mail to Steeple Hill Reader Service:
IN U.S.A.: P.O. Box 1867, Buffalo, NY 14240-1867
IN CANADA: P.O. Box 609, Fort Erie, Ontario L2A 5X3
Not valid to current subscribers of Love Inspired books.

Want to try two free books from another series?
Call 1-800-873-8635 or visit www.morefreebooks.com

* Terms and prices subject to change without notice. Prices do not include applicable taxes. Sales tax applicable in N.Y. Canadian residents will be charged applicable provincial taxes and GST. Offer not valid in Quebec. This offer is limited to one order per household. All orders subject to approval. Credit or debit balances in a customer's account(s) may be offset by any other outstanding balance owed by or to the customer. Please allow 4 to 6 weeks for delivery. Offer available while quantities last.

Your Privacy: Steeple Hill Books is committed to protecting your privacy. Our Privacy Policy is available online at www.SteepleHill.com or upon request from the Reader Service. From time to time we make our lists of customers available to reputable third parties who may have a product or service of interest to you. If you would prefer we not share your name and address, please check here. ☐

LIREG09

Love Inspired

TITLES AVAILABLE NEXT MONTH
Available October 27, 2009

TOGETHER FOR THE HOLIDAYS by Margaret Daley
Fostered by Love
Single mother Lisa Morgan only wants to raise her son with love and
good values. Yet when a world-weary cop becomes the boy's reluctant
father figure, Lisa discovers she has a Christmas wish as well....

A FAMILY FOR THANKSGIVING by Patricia Davids
After the Storm
Nicki Appleton may have to say goodbye to the sweet toddler she
took in after the tornado. Yet when the man she once loved comes
home to High Plains, can she count on Clay Logan to be her family for
Thanksgiving—and forever?

CLOSE TO HOME by Carolyne Aarsen
Jace Scholte was the town bad boy—until he fell for Dodie Westerveld
But instead of marrying him, Dodie ran away without a word. Now,
they're both back in town. But Dodie still won't talk about the past....

BLESSINGS OF THE SEASON by Annie Jones and Brenda Minton
Two heartwarming holiday stories.
In "The Holiday Husband," Addie McCoy's holidays have never
been traditional. Could Nate Browder be the perfect old-fashioned
husband? In "The Christmas Letter," single mom Isabella Grant's
dreams of family come true when a handsome soldier comes knocking
on her door!

HIS COWGIRL BRIDE by Debra Clopton
Former bronc rider Brent Stockwell doesn't think *ladies* belong in the
pen or his life. But cowgirl Tacy Jones has come to Mule Hollow to
train wild horses and she's determined to change his mind—and his
heart.

A FOREVER CHRISTMAS by Missy Tippens
Busy single dad Gregory Jones doesn't have much time to spend
with his sons. When Sarah Radcliffe tries to teach him that love and
attention are the greatest Christmas gifts of all, will he realize his love
is the perfect gift for Sarah as well?

LICNMBPA1009